The Wrong Way to Use Healing Magic
Vol. 2
KUROKATA
ONE PEACE BOOKS
T0019071

Character Introductions

Usato

Amako

Kazuki
Aruku
Suzune
Welcie
Blurin

Gladys

“Allow me to welcome you all to Luqvist.”

Halpha

Felm

Rose

CONTENTS

Rescue Team Guidelines:
Stance on training

- There will be no mercy.
- You will train harder than any orders you are given.
- The training will be hell.

CHAPTER 1

Unhinged?! The Black Knight Appears!

I leaped into the heart of battle. I was a member of the Rescue Team: healing the injured with my magic and saving those on the brink of death. I felt the distinct fear that each decision might be my last. I ran through the battlefield, helping those in need and carrying an injured knight, when—

"Whoa?!"

The demons had used a wounded soldier as a trap to lure me in, and I'd stepped smack bang right in the middle of it. As I hefted an unconscious soldier under each arm, the surrounding demons focused their attacks directly on me. They launched fireballs, sent earthen spears thrusting up from the ground, and fired bullets of water. I slipped and dodged the attacks with everything I had, all the while working my healing magic on the soldiers in my arms.

"What the hell is he?!" cried one demon.

"He doesn't move like a human! I can't hit him!" shouted another.

"Wait, don't tell me . . . is this one of the monsters that commander Vergrett mentioned?!"

Are they seriously just chatting while they have me surrounded?!

Whatever. I didn't go through all that training just to die in a dumb trap!

"Coming through!" I shouted.

With my arms and legs wrapped in healing magic, I weaved past the demons' magical attacks and launched a kick at the nearest one to create an opening.

"Hurk!"

The demon flew across the ground, rolling to a stop a few meters away, completely unconscious. The other demons froze in shock at the sight of their comrade, broken with a single kick.

Now's my chance!

I leaped into the air and off the shoulders of an ogling demon, breaking free of the trap. The demons were in disarray, but they still tried to give chase. I shot them a brief glance before breaking into a full sprint. They didn't have a chance of catching me, and their angry shouts faded as the distance between us widened.

I passed the still unconscious knights I'd been carrying to some men in the rearguard, then took a breath and leaped back into the fray.

"This is brutal," I muttered.

I frowned, looking for someone to aid, surrounded by the stench of blood. Around me were the fallen, both knights and demons alike. My ears rang with screams and the clashing of weapons.

This place is hell.

There was no other place that so perfectly epitomized the

word "bloodbath." And yet here I was, fighting at the heart of it. But I wasn't here as a knight, battling to fell my enemies. I was part of the Rescue Team, battling to save lives.

And I didn't have time to tremble with fear.

"The battle rages on," I muttered, picking up my pace.

I was determined; I would be strong in the face of this war.

I saw a knight, his face twisted in pain. I saw a demon standing before him, blade in hand, readying a finishing blow. I moved with blinding speed, weaving through the knights and the demons, rushing to the injured man's aid. Blood poured from his leg. He had nowhere left to run.

"Not while I still stand . . ." I whispered.

I took a deep breath and kicked hard off the ground, leaping forward. Every fiber of my being was focused on saving the life that was about to end in front of my eyes.

* * *

The battle between Llinger Kingdom and the Demon Lord's army was a harsh, savage thing to behold, especially for those of us who'd been summoned from somewhere considerably more peaceful.

The stench of blood, the feel of enemies falling to my sword—I couldn't stand it. It was a feeling that went beyond mere description, but Kazuki-kun and I were the heroes of

Llinger Kingdom now. We trudged past the corpses and continued onward.

The Demon Lord's army had a slight upper hand. If we could push through their main forces and take down their commanding officer, it would mean victory for Llinger Kingdom.

But we had an ocean of demons to get through first.

"Senpai!"

At Kazuki-kun's shout, I realized that a demon had crept up behind me, his spear at the ready. I twisted as he thrust his blade, dodging the blow. I sent the tip of his spear flying with a slice of my sword. The demon clicked his tongue in frustration as I pushed my palm toward him and unleashed a lightning strike.

"Hah!"

The lightning fired at the sound of my battle cry, passing through the demon that stood before me and striking those at the ready behind him.

But it didn't matter if I could control lightning, and it didn't matter whether or not I was a hero—if I was caught off guard again, it could spell my doom.

"Heroes!" said the knight captain, running up to Kazuki-kun and me to give a status update. "We've cleared the enemies in the surrounding area."

"Make sure the injured are taken to the rearguard. The rest of us will continue to push forward," I told him.

"Understood!"

I watched as the knight captain left to relay my orders. Then I surveyed the battlefield. Around us were the scattered bodies of the demons that had tried to kill us.

"They're invaders now, but they had lives once, just like us . . ." I began.

To say I could take a life without feeling its weight was a lie, but that alone was not enough of a reason to put my friends and my allies in danger. I would keep pushing forward.

We would keep pushing forward.

"Looks like we're clear of enemies here," said Kazuki-kun, sheathing his sword and walking over to me.

"Yes," I said, roused from my thoughts. "But their main base, their headquarters, is still some distance away. And we're not clear of the danger here either."

"Oh. Yep."

A giant snake, a monster, was running rampant in another part of the battlefield, a little ways from us. It was injuring and wounding a great many knights, enough that I wanted to run in to provide support. But I knew, at the same time, that if Kazuki-kun and I left our current position, ultimate victory for Llinger would only grow more distant.

"Senpai, we have to hurry!" said Kazuki-kun. "We'll do what we have to, then come back and kill that snake!"

"Good call. Let's do what we came here to do."

I looked out over the knights behind us, all of whom had come on the knight captain's order. We'd taken noticeable losses since the start of the battle. Fortunately, the fallen knights were carried away at blistering speed by the Rescue Team, and with Kazuki-kun and I constantly pushing forward, we had yet to see any casualties.

"Knights," I said, "prepare to move onwa—"

But before I could finish giving my order, I felt a sudden, indescribable chill and heard the shuffle of heavy metal drawing closer.

"Found you."

The voice felt entirely too quiet for the battlefield. It belonged to something in a pitch-black set of armor, dark as any shadow. The something in the armor had come with demon reinforcements, and it weaved through them until it stood before us.

I felt hatred boil in me the very moment I saw it. I glimpsed two eyes peeking from a slit in its polished black helmet. As I did, I felt my hand instinctively grip the handle of my sword tighter.

"Everyone, stop!" I said, barking an order at the knights behind me. "Don't move."

I didn't want them to do anything rash. I set my mind on keeping calm—and on keeping the fear in my heart at bay.

"What . . . is that?" Kazuki-kun asked, his voice quivering.

"I don't have the slightest idea," I said. "But one thing's for certain: it's unlike any demon we've seen so far."

The black knight sized us up silently. The glossy black armor that surrounded its body crawled as if it were a living organism. I wanted nothing more than to kill it immediately, but my instincts held me back, ringing like an alarm bell in my head.

As I watched the black knight, thinking about how best to approach it, several knights launched themselves from behind me, ignoring my order.

"No! Wait!" I cried.

But the knight captain and the knights with him could no longer stand the pressure emanating from this shadowy foe. Hate welled in their eyes and they launched themselves at the black knight with fierce battle cries.

Kazuki-kun and I hurriedly stopped the remaining knights from attacking, then called out again to the knight captain and his men.

"All of you, stop!"

But they were beyond listening to our commands. They continued to close in. However, the black knight and its surrounding demon forces didn't move. Their calm and complete disregard in the face of the incoming knights worried me. One of the knights reached the black knight and raised his sword.

"Eat this!" he shouted, bringing his heavy blade down in an attack.

The sword sliced deep into the black knight's armor. It was a fatal blow. But still, the black knight remained still, unmoving, its creepy black armor crawling around its body. Another knight followed quickly behind the first, his voice an enraged roar as he ran his spear straight through the black knight.

"You will fall!" he shouted.

Then the knight captain pointed his great sword at the black knight and readied his own attack. The blade must have been at least as big as he was. The captain rushed in at a speed that belied his powerful frame. His power and skill were the real deal. Regardless of whatever it was that had spurred on his rash attack, there was no denying that with his experience in the Llinger army and his raw abilities, he was a true warrior.

The savage thrust was as powerful as a tank, and it sunk the sword into the black knight's body, which was already pierced with two spears. The knight captain glared at the black knight as he pushed the great sword in even deeper.

"Whatever magic it is you intend to use, you will die before you ever get a chance to—"

"Hmph. You think that *this* is enough to kill me?" said the black knight. The voice that spoke was flat and lifeless. It was impossible to tell if it was male or female. It scratched at the hearts of those who heard it, filling them with unease. "You, them . . . you're no different than all the other trash."

"What did you say?"

"You're in my way," said the black knight. "Move."

The black armor contorted wildly, and its chest plate transformed into a spike. It went straight for the knight captain.

"What?!"

The knight captain released his great sword and leaped backward to safety.

"Captain!" cried the knights still surrounding the black knight.

But their captain had escaped danger and drew from his hip another sword.

"Be on guard!" he shouted to his men. "We haven't felled it yet! We will surround it and finish it off!"

"Yes, sir!"

Kazuki-kun couldn't bear to stand by and just watch.

"Senpai! I'll back them up!" he said, racing off toward the knight captain.

"Kazuki-kun, wait!" I said. I let out a frustrated grunt when he didn't listen and turned to the troops. "Everyone, follow me!"

I'm glad to see that Kazuki-kun is more assertive than he was back at home, but there's a difference between being courageous and being foolhardy!

I took off after him with the remaining knights in tow.

In a way, this was a chance for us. Our enemy was badly wounded from the knights that had struck first. Unless it had a healer on hand or was invincible, it didn't stand a chance.

"Let's see if you humans are worthy of my time," said the black knight, pulling the great sword and spears from its body. It seemed utterly bored with the knight captain and his men as it flicked its wrist and uttered a single word.

"Reflect."

Blood burst into the air. It came from the knight captain and his three men, all of whom collapsed where they stood like puppets with their strings cut.

"What?!" I exclaimed.

The black knight had done nothing that even looked like an attack. There were no traces of any magic use. In the literal blink of an eye, four battle-hardened knights had been left in pools of their own blood.

"Senpai . . . what *was* that?" asked Kazuki-kun.

He was frozen by the brutal sight that now met his eyes, his hands shaking.

"I don't know," I said. "But charging in recklessly is a bad idea . . ."

I couldn't make heads or tails of it. Was it possible that the black knight had moved faster than we could see? Did it draw its sword and attack the knights? Or had it unleashed razor-sharp wind magic?

Whatever the case, it was stupid to approach without a plan.

"Seems like the only ones capable of handling a foe like this . . . are us," I said.

"Looks like it," Kazuki-kun agreed.

"Don't tell me this is all you've got?" muttered the black knight, its eyes firmly on us as targets. "Please tell me this isn't where it ends."

But this was good for us. So long as the black knight had us in its sights, the knights behind us wouldn't come to harm.

"Knights," I said, careful not to take my eyes off the black knight as I shouted orders. "Can we rely on you to handle the surrounding demon forces? We need you to keep them occupied and hang on long enough for us to take this black knight down."

"Leave it to us, heroes! We'll see your orders through or die trying!"

I chuckled.

"That's the spirit," I said.

Now I knew we could fight without fear of being ambushed. I readied my sword and stood next to Kazuki-kun. The black knight remained ever motionless before us.

Is it simply a show of bravado? Or does this knight not have a fighting stance to begin with?

"I'll go first," Kazuki-kun stated.

"We still don't know enough about our enemy. Kazuki-kun, don't attack it directly with your magic," I said, then turned to the knights. "As soon as Kazuki unleashes his spell, move in on the demons."

"Understood!"

Kazuki-kun held his sword in his left hand as he raised his right palm toward the black knight. While my lightning magic was great for area-of-effect damage, Kazuki-kun's magic was better suited to a single point of attack. He turned his magic into a ball of light. It was deadly accurate and contained powerful piercing strength.

"However quick you are, you can't outrun light!" he yelled.

The ball of light flew from Kazuki-kun's palm straight toward the black knight. There was no dodging it. The magic struck the black knight in the left shoulder, and smoke rose from the point of impact, a side effect of the light magic's purifying effects.

"Hmph. Interesting," said the black knight before giving orders to the demons waiting behind it. "Take care of the knights."

Even now, the black knight showed no signs of being hurt. The damage to its armor from the knight captain's attacks had also disappeared entirely.

Light magic should be its weakness. What is going on?

"It's no good," said Kazuki-kun. "My light magic doesn't work."

"Light . . . Quite the rare type, that," said the black knight. "I've never faced it before. How intriguing. Reflect."

It spoke the exact same word it spoke when the knight captain fell.

Reflect? What does it mean?

Suddenly, Kazuki-kun collapsed to his knees, clutching his left shoulder as he screamed in pain.

"What's wrong?!" I shouted.

"It's my shoulder. It's . . . like it's burning . . ."

"Your shoulder?"

Blood dripped from the gaps in his armor around his shoulder.

What happened?! Was something fired into the gaps in the armor?! But I didn't see anything like that! This is . . .

"A direct attack . . . under the armor?" I asked.

Kazuki-kun cast first aid magic on his shoulder.

"I'm okay," he said.

But I knew that his first aid was little more than a stopgap solution. It was like putting disinfectant and a Band-Aid on a wound that needed stitches. With enough time, he'd be able to heal himself to almost full health, but—

"Look out!" I yelled.

A mass of black swiped at the two of us, and I blocked it with the flat of my sword. The black shape had come from the black knight's arm. It was less like armor and more like a tentacle or feeler, and the sight of it made me feel sick as it slunk back into the black knight's body.

So it can change shape in order to attack too? This is bad. We still haven't figured out how it works yet.

"Such a pity," murmured the black knight.

"What is? What do you mean?" I shot back.

The black knight chuckled.

"What, indeed."

Easily as creepy as it is dangerous.

It felt like we were facing off against a monster that wasn't of this world.

* * *

I weaved into the midst of the battle. The battlefield was a mess of friends and foes, and at their feet were the bodies of the fallen and the dead. I did my utmost to heal the injured. Wiping the sweat from my brow with my sleeve, I felt the heavy pressure of being in the midst of war.

"Please try not to overdo it," I said as I healed one knight, already looking for the next in need of aid.

The stench of death wafted up around me, and I held back the urge to vomit. I kept moving forward.

"You knew this was what it would be like," I muttered to myself.

I knew that death thrived on the battlefield. I knew that I might fall here and breathe my last. I knew it, but I would not fall back. I was a healer and a part of the Rescue Team. It was my responsibility to help those who fought.

And besides, I'd made a promise. I would protect them all: the kingdom we now called home, and my friends.

That's why I—

But before I could finish the thought, my head was assaulted by searing pain. At the same time, I saw an image like a still frame flash before my eyes. I saw Inukami-senpai and Kazuki being killed.

I cast my healing magic, but the pain refused to recede, the vision never leaving my sight.

"Dammit . . . What the hell . . ." I muttered.

"You stop and you die!" cried a demon who saw me writhing and took it as a golden opportunity to slice me down with its ax.

"No! Not here!" I yelled.

I rolled to avoid the blow, but the ax gouged into my right arm, slicing it open. A grunt escaped my gritted teeth. The wound wasn't anything to worry about, but my head still felt like it was going to split open.

What is this? Are Inukami-senpai and Kazuki in some kind of danger?

I left the demon where he stood and tried to run, but my vision wavered and I tripped over a corpse, tumbling to the ground.

"Die!" the demon growled, bringing its ax down for a second time.

I couldn't heal an attack that killed on impact. That was impossible. If I died here, Kazuki and Inukami-senpai would be helpless. I'd never get to them. I raised my arms, prepared to lose them in order to defend my head, and braced for impact.

"You will not touch him, demon!" someone shouted.

"Hurk?!" the demon grunted.

The ax-wielding demon was sent flying to the ground. I lowered my arms to find a knight where the demon once stood, sword in hand.

"Are you okay?!" he asked.

"Huh. Wait. Y-You're the knight from before . . ."

I'd saved his life. I'd never thought he'd be back to return the favor.

Without him, I might have died.

I let out a sigh of relief, then suddenly remembered what I'd seen. The aching in my head began to subside.

"Oh no! Inuka—I mean, the heroes! Do you know where they are?"

"The heroes? They're at the front lines, but—"

"Got it! Thanks!" I said, taking off into a sprint.

"B-Be careful!"

"You too!"

The front lines weren't too far from where I was.

And if what I saw through my headache was a premonition, then there was no time to lose.

"Please, guys, be safe . . ."

* * *

"Come now, what are you waiting for?" said the black knight, goading us. "Don't tell me you're afraid . . . already?"

I grit my teeth. This was no time for acting rash.

"Senpai . . ."

"Cool it, Kazuki-kun. We don't want to move in unprepared."

The attack to Kazuki-kun's shoulder had struck without touching his armor or the clothing underneath it. The bloody wounds of the fallen knights, too, somehow opened *underneath* their clothes. With one eye still on the black knight, I took better stock of the injured knights. One looked as if he'd been cut, and two appeared to have suffered stab wounds. The knight captain, too, had been run through by a blade.

"And then Kazuki-kun . . ." I muttered.

Just like that, everything clicked into place.

Everyone's injuries reflect the very attacks they launched on the black knight!

That was why, when the black knight had attacked earlier, it had uttered the words, "Such a pity."

It was because—

"That armor," I said, "it reflects any attack back on the attacker."

"Well, aren't you the smart one," said the black knight. "Nobody else has worked it out quite so quickly."

But it doesn't even seem to care that I understand how the armor works. The black knight is still convinced it has the upper hand.

And for now, that was true. I still didn't have a strategy for countering the armor. I had to assume that the black knight's armor would also reflect blunt weapons. Blades were of course out of the question. The armor reflected any and every attack. We didn't have any real choice but to avoid battling the black knight entirely.

"Don't think that running is an option," said the black knight. "It's not. You two are much stronger than the others, so I'll make you struggle, and flail, and suffer, and then watch you die."

"Then we don't have any other choice," I said. "We fight. The other knights don't stand a chance against this thing."

"But, senpai, If the black knight really does reflect any attack, how do we kill it?"

"Kazuki-kun. There's something I want to try but it's kind of reckless."

My guess was that because the black knight uttered the word "reflect," there were certain conditions that had to be met for its counterattacks to work. If that was true, I wanted to find out exactly where we could attack from—that meant using non-lethal blows and attacking with light gashes until we discovered a weak point.

I whispered the idea into Kazuki-kun's ear and explained my strategy. Then I had the knights behind us ready to handle the periphery.

"Senpai," Kazuki-kun said, frowning, "that's *way* too dangerous . . ."

"Hah!" I said with a grin. "If worse comes to worst, we'll just get Usato to heal us."

Kazuki-kun sighed as I readied my sword.

"I just *knew* you were going to say something like that."

Kazuki-kun was the key to my strategy working. I had to support him at every turn.

"Let's get to it, then!" I said.

I dashed at the black knight, with Kazuki-kun close behind.

"Hmph. Still intent on meeting your deaths. You should know better," said the black knight.

"Like we were ever going to back down!" I quipped.

The black knight morphed its armor into another piercing feeler thing, which stretched out and aimed right for us. Attacking it would only mean attacking ourselves, so we ducked under it. At the same time, I cast a ball of lightning in my hand and pitched it at the black knight's feet.

"Can't stop this though, can you?" I said.

Dust flew up into the air with a flash, clouding the black knight's vision. Moving within the cover of dust, Kazuki-kun and I launched our sneak attack, just as we planned. If it worked, we'd know that what it couldn't see *could* hurt it.

I kept completely silent as I sliced at the black knight's shoulder. Then I spun behind it and cut a shallow slash in a diagonal line along its back. In the next instant, I felt heat run through my shoulder, followed by warm blood spreading under my armor.

"Gr . . . I guess that didn't work," I muttered.

And from the blood flowing from Kazuki-kun's cheek, I could see that his attack didn't work either.

The black knight burst into laughter.

"Kazuki-kun!" I shouted.

"Senpai!"

We couldn't run, but we couldn't fight back. The situation felt hopeless. Maybe Usato-kun could have kept fighting, injury after injury, but we weren't used to dealing with such pain, and we felt stuck in place.

"I guess I'm just no different from any other ordinary human," I muttered.

In the world that I came from, I'd never been dealt a wound like this. My shoulder hurt so bad I had to hold back the tears.

"Wait. My shoulder . . . ?"

I'd hit the black knight with two attacks—one to its shoulder and one to its back. So why didn't my back pulse with a similar pain? Why hadn't that attack been reflected? Kazuki-kun and I had attacked at the same time. My first attack opened our offense, but I launched my second *at the same time* as Kazuki-kun's.

But only his attack had been properly reflected.

"Is it possible . . . ? Kazuki-kun!" I shouted. "One more time! Attack!"

I sent lightning flowing to my feet.

"Bu——Okay! I'm on it!"

Kazuki-kun saw me crouched, then faced the black knight again. He didn't know what I had planned, but he did as I asked. He was nothing if not the very height of reliability.

This might be our only chance. Come on, Kazuki-kun!

"Is your friend too scared to play?" teased the black knight.

"Shut it!"

More darkness flew out from the black knight to attack Kazuki-kun, but he parried it with the flat of his sword.

"Try this!" said the black knight.

Kazuki-kun grunted as the black mass hit his sword hard, like a hammer. But it didn't stop him, and he closed in on the black knight.

Not yet, not yet. You need to draw it in further.

I gripped the sword tight in my right hand and saw it in my mind—saw myself moving faster than anybody else, so overwhelmingly fast that I couldn't be stopped. The lightning gathering at my feet crackled, sending sparks flashing across the ground. Kazuki-kun glanced at me briefly and saw what I was planning, then put the sword he'd been using for defense in its scabbard.

The black knight tilted its head, confused by Kazuki-kun's odd decision, but Kazuki-kun ignored it, gathering light in his hands before slamming them together like a powerful clap.

"Got you!" he said.

A brilliant light filled the immediate area. The black knight responded just as Kazuki-kun expected, lifting its arms to shield its eyes.

"Now," I whispered.

With the black knight blinded and its attention taken away from me, I had my chance. I released the magic charged in my legs and dove. My abilities were energized by the lightning magic, and I quickly passed Kazuki-kun and closed in on the black knight.

Still, I knew a frontal attack was useless. Even blinded, the black knight had lost none of its power, and I couldn't let Kazuki-kun's decoy attack be for nothing. I stopped in place and spun quickly to the black knight's back.

The black knight laughed.

"Blinding your opponent. Quite the textbook strategy!"

The black knight still hadn't noticed that I'd moved behind it. I gripped my sword and ran it through the black knight's back with everything I had. The black knight's laughter vanished as the sword pushed inside of it.

"What . . . the . . . ?" the black knight uttered.

"It hasn't been reflected," I said. "Does that mean . . . this works?"

When I'd attacked the black knight, only the attack to its back had gone unreflected. I predicted that this was because the black knight hadn't been aware of it. So I put my theory to the test by getting to its back and catching it by surprise. It was a dangerous bet, but my attack still hadn't been reflected.

"Did it work?" I asked.

Kazuki-kun went completely pale at the sight of me running my sword through the black knight's back but quickly became aware of the impact. The black knight coughed, still impaled, and spat a chunk of something black from the mouth area of its helmet.

"It worked?!" Kazuki-kun asked.

I saw black liquid dripping from the black knight's armor. I was sure my sword had hurt it. I drove it in even deeper.

"Kazuki-kun!" I shouted. "Now! Your attacks will work!"

Kazuki-kun leaped in with a battle cry.

"How . . . ? No . . ." spat the black knight. "Not here . . . not like . . . this. Not . . ."

If we killed the black knight, we would make a huge dent in the demon forces, and their morale would plummet. The tide of battle would quickly turn in our favor. Kazuki-kun neared the black knight, channeling all his strength into his sword, everything he had in a decisive, killing strike, when—

"Not . . . ever," said the black knight, its voice dripping with derision.

I felt a fierce pain shoot through my chest.

"Huh?" I exclaimed.

Blood stained my clothes through the gaps in my armor. It bubbled up into my mouth. I released my sword and fell to my knees, unable to stand. As I struggled to grasp what had just happened, blood splashed across my cheek.

"No, Kazuki-kun!"

I looked up to see Kazuki-kun impaled on the black knight's sword. He was slumped there, his sword still held high. The black knight let loose a terrifying laugh.

"W-Why?"

The black knight turned to look down at me.

"You thought your attacks could harm me. That was a mistake. This armor is my magic. It is *me.* It is all-powerful, and nothing can hurt what lies within it. The reflection isn't automatic—I *choose* when to use it. It doesn't matter if I see an attack, feel it, or realize that it's happening. None of that matters at all."

What even is that?

The black knight is a monster like no other.

Nobody even stands a chance.

I put a hand to my chest, blood still flowing from my wound, and collapsed in a heap. A pool of red spread out underneath me, wetting my cheek. My body grew weak, and my consciousness began to fade. And the words that left my lips were, strangely, an apology to a person who wasn't even here.

"I'm so sorry . . . Usato . . . kun," I whispered.

* * *

I looked down at the fallen heroes, then surveyed the battlefield. The morale of the Llinger knights was broken, crumbling as the demons grew more confident. It was simple, and I suppose simple was good enough. All the same, I could not help but wonder what it was we would ultimately earn with this battle.

"What did the Demon Lord have in mind, sending us out to this battle?" I pondered. "If it was territory he wanted, there were better ways to take it . . . Hm. In any case, it is no bother of mine."

The two heroes had seemed like worthy foes, but now they were little more than disgraced heaps before me. I saw nothing more of value in this battle.

It was always like this.

Since the day I was born, none could hurt me. Neither demon nor human—not even my parents.

All of them had died, just as these heroes would.

"And so it ends . . ."

I put my sword in my opposite hand and turned to the female. There was still breath in her yet. She held a hand to her chest as she struggled to glare at me. I did not care. I aimed my blade at her heart. It would not miss its target.

"You provided me some enjoyment, human," I said.

And then I brought my sword down.

"Not on my watch!"

The shout of a youthful voice rang in my ears.

"Hngh?"

I let out something of a stupid grunt in surprise, and as I turned to the sound, a force unlike anything I had ever felt slammed into my cheek.

"Ouch!"

CHAPTER 2

Bam! The Healing Punch!

My head went completely blank. I was confronted by the exact sight I'd already seen: Inukami-senpai and Kazuki collapsed on the ground, the knight in black armor preparing to finish them off for good.

"Am I too late?! No, there's still time!" I yelled.

Once I sent the black knight flying with my strike, I rushed to Inukami-senpai and Kazuki and started healing them. Inukami-senpai had been stabbed in the back and through her chest. Kazuki had a similar wound, like he'd been impaled on a blade.

The wounds were fatal.

Or at least, they would have been if it wasn't for me. I could heal any wound they suffered so long as they still drew breath.

"U-Usato-kun . . . I never thought . . . you'd come to me in a dream as I lay dying . . . Just once, would you . . . call me . . . Suzu-tan . . . ?"

"You're in better shape than I thought, Inukami-senpai. I'm going to heal Kazuki first."

"Wa-Wait. Wait. Better shape . . . ? I have a hole in me . . ."

Girl gets run through with a sword and still has time for jokes? Is she for real? Talk about a turn-off.

But it *was* true that her wound was deep. Fortunately, not so deep I couldn't heal it. I moved on to Kazuki, who was still unconscious. I had to heal him too, but—

"Usato-kun! Behind you!"

I reflexively hefted Inukami-senpai and Kazuki into my arms and leaped away. I sent healing magic pulsing through my arms and looked behind me. The black knight had brought its sword down right where I had stood. I felt a cold trickle of sweat run down my back—a moment later and I'd have been dead.

"Th-That was too close for comfort! Thanks, senpai."

"Don't mention it. Worth it for a chance to be carried in your arms."

"Does anything faze you?"

It looked like she was healed enough that she could speak, but her comment felt entirely unsuited to the battlefield.

The black knight stood with its sword still in the ground. It let out a roar not unlike a wild beast.

"Huh?" I said.

The black knight raised its head to face me.

"Who the hell are you?!" it shouted.

"Your helmet, it . . ."

The side of the helmet I'd punched had crumbled away, showing half of the face hidden behind it. It had the tanned skin and silver hair unique to demons, but the features were that of a young girl.

"That massive knight is female?!" I asked.

Anybody would have assumed that the wearer of the black

armor was a giant of a man. I turned to Inukami-senpai, whose expression was one of shock.

"You hurt it . . ." she muttered.

Wait. That's *what you're surprised about?! That I hurt it?*

Is the black knight special or something?

"Uh, sorry, but can you get me up to speed on what's going on?" I asked.

"Huh? Oh, right. Of course. You don't know."

Inukami-senpai explained the black knight's abilities to me. Apparently, the knight used a crazy magic that reflected any attack on her armor back onto her attacker. Inukami-senpai, Kazuki, the knights—they'd all fallen to the armor's power, unable to counter it.

"The hell?" I said. "That's gotta be against the rules, no?"

Still wary of our main foe, I glanced at the fallen Llinger knights. They were in bad shape, but they were still breathing. I could still save them. I had to hand it to the knights of this world—they were survivors.

I lowered senpai and Kazuki to the ground; their wounds were mostly healed.

As I watched the black knight, her black armor grew stranger the longer I looked at it. If it was constructed by magic, then it was likely dark magic. I tried to remember what was written about it in the book that Rose gave me. If I recalled correctly, it wasn't just rare—dark magic offered very unique powers and was far better suited to battle than any other magic types.

I stepped away from Inukami-senpai and Kazuki. I wanted to keep them out of it.

The black knight put a hand to her red, swollen cheek. Her face twitched with a mix of emotions, and then she began to cackle with laughter.

Oh, man, she's crazy. And not crazy like Inukami-senpai is crazy. First I fight a bear, then a snake, now a lunatic. Am I ever going to fight a normal person or what?

I didn't want to fight, but I had to do something, and I had to do it quickly if I wanted to save the fallen knights. I took a step forward, enveloping my body in healing magic.

"Usato-kun?!"

"I'll take care of this," I said. "In the meantime, use your first aid magic to keep those knights on life support."

If the black knight reflected attacks back at me, it didn't matter. I could heal my own injuries. But I had to render it powerless, which meant either throwing it somewhere far into the distance or tying it down.

"S-Stop!" cried Inukami-senpai as I leaped toward the black knight. "You don't stand a chance!"

The black knight morphed her armor into a huge arm and swung it at me, but the attack was one-note—far too basic. It was meant to draw an attack from the enemy that could be reflected. And maybe that was what would happen, but the pain wouldn't bother me. I launched a right kick and felt a sickly slimy sensation on the sole of my boot as I sent the arm flying.

My foot, it doesn't hurt. Did she not reflect it?

"What?!" shouted the black knight.

I couldn't understand why she was shocked when *she* was the one doing the attacking. Still, I didn't feel even a sliver of pain.

Something isn't right. She can't possibly be out of magic already. Perhaps she didn't use reflect this time.

The giant arm swung at me again. I parried the blow and got closer to the black knight, using a spin kick to knock the arm out of my path. It wobbled like an octopus tentacle and I crushed it under my foot, closing in even closer to the black knight.

"Take this!"

I spun and launched a right hook at the black knight with enough force to send her arm flying. But the right hook was just to put the black knight where I wanted her. The real strike was my left! She didn't even try to defend and simply ate my left punch with a sputter.

"Huh?" I muttered.

Is this really as strong as she gets? She's all wobbly on her feet already.

But I had to assume that this might be part of the black knight's strategy. For all I knew, she was luring me into a false sense of security so she could launch a surprise attack. I wasn't doing any heavy damage with my attacks wrapped in healing magic, so I saw right through her act.

I reached up and grabbed the black knight by her neck, looking to throw her to the ground. Suddenly, however, the solid sensation of her armor disappeared under my grasp.

"Huh?! Whoa!"

I looked at my hand, from which a muddy black liquid bubbled and spilled.

What the hell is this armor?! I don't get it!

"Oop!" I sputtered, noticing the black knight's other hand flying toward me.

I leaped back to where Inukami-senpai was. If I couldn't grab ahold of the black knight, that meant throwing her was no longer an option.

The only thing left was to stop her, restrain her somehow. That meant giving her a good smack to dull her senses first.

"Inukami-senpai, do we have something to bind the black knight with?" I asked.

"Nothing at hand, but . . . why?"

"I want to tie her up."

Uh-oh. I can see by that look on her face that she's getting entirely the wrong idea.

"Yeah, no," I said. "I'm not into bondage."

"At least let me say something before you jump to conclusions."

"Guess I'll have to think of something else."

I turned to face the black knight, healing magic wrapping around me as I clenched my fists.

"Let's do this," I whispered.

My coat flew out behind me as I launched myself at the black knight. In response, she morphed her armor into tentacle-like weapons and sent them straight at me.

"Die!" she shouted.

"Not even if you asked nicely!"

I twisted my body and dodged one of her attacks. I weaved past the ones I could and knocked the others away with my hand. Her attacks were much slower than I expected. I could easily handle even more than this.

The black knight shouted, enraged, and created a huge arm with a sharp spike at the front of it. It was a brutal-looking weapon. She drew the spike in and then fired it like a bullet.

"Take this!" she shouted.

I'm moving too fast toward her now. I won't be able to get out of the way.

"If I can't dodge it, then I've got no other choice!"

I thrust my palm out in front of my face to meet the black knight's attack head-on. Blood burst from my hand as the spike ran right through it. I clenched my teeth hard, gritting through the pain, then grabbed ahold of the black knight's giant arm and pulled it as hard as I could.

"Huh?!" she grunted.

The black knight was pulled off balance, but her glare remained locked on me. She unsheathed her sword and swung it at me even as she was pulled out of her stance.

"Whoa?!" I cried, bending my body sideways to dodge the blade coming straight for my head.

No healing for the headless! Gotta be careful! But—

"I'll never let you hit me!" I shouted.

I weaved under the swipe of the black knight's sword and launched an elbow into her side, which she'd left open. It was a light attack, and one I knew wouldn't slow me down even if it was reflected. I didn't expect it to have much of an impact, but . . .

"Oof!" she grunted.

"She's hurt?!"

The black knight took a step backward, wobbling on her feet. I couldn't understand why she was reeling from my attack. But I didn't have time to linger on the thought—I needed to bring her down quickly or I'd never heal the knights in time.

"Let's end this," I said, wrapping my fist in healing magic.

I readied myself for another round, then jumped in.

* * *

I simply couldn't believe my eyes. Couldn't believe what I was seeing. Usato-kun, wrapped in healing magic, was pushing the black knight back. It was completely one-sided. When the black knight tried to attack with her armor, it was deflected. When she swung her sword, her attacks were quickly evaded.

The black knight didn't know how to fight. Her attacks were easy to follow, and even the knight captain—whom I kept on life support with first aid magic—could have easily taken her down. But what made the black knight terrifying was not her fighting ability; it was the magic that allowed her to reflect any attack.

And yet here was Usato-kun, in the face of this impenetrable magic, landing punch after punch on the black knight as if it were nothing.

Usato-kun grunted as he launched a kick. The black knight heaved as she took the shot, the attack easily breaking the black clump she'd put up to defend herself. But even then, Usato-kun never looked as if he felt his own hits reflected back at him.

I couldn't understand it. The magic of the black knight's armor was still at work, but for some reason, it had no effect on Usato-kun.

Why is Usato-kun using his healing magic, anyway?

I knew that he used his healing magic to stave off exhaustion, but he had the healing magic encircling his fists and feet too.

Doesn't that mean that with every attack, he's healing the black knight?

"No way," I stated out loud.

Is there something about Usato-kun's healing magic that counters the black knight's own magic?

Whenever the black knight launched a feeler at Usato-kun, it was countered by a strike of some kind and its form crumbled into a kind of sludge. Usato-kun didn't seem to notice it himself, but every time he hit the armor, the healing light around his arms dimmed noticeably for an instant.

That can only mean that—

"The black armor's weakness is healing magic," I stated.

Perhaps, I mused, some unique property of the black knight's armor was allowing for Usato-kun's attacks to break through her otherwise impenetrable armor. I tried to think. For attacks to be reflected, the black armor needed to be damaged. That meant blunt-force attacks, slices, and stabbing. All of them left damage. And as long as the black knight was aware of that damage, she could fire it back at the attacker. I'd felt it firsthand.

However you looked at it, the black armor was incredibly dangerous, even invincible.

And yet it had a weakness.

"It's healing magic," I repeated.

Usato-kun landed a heavy chop on the black knight's

shoulder with a furious glare, then slammed a palm into the black knight's stomach, doubling her over.

Healing magic gave its caster the ability to heal the wounds of living creatures. But those who awoke to the power couldn't use non-elemental magic—that meant no attack magic. As far as I could tell, the black knight's armor wasn't registering Usato-kun's fists as damage.

But right now, it didn't matter why Usato-kun was using his healing magic—it only mattered that whenever the magic came in contact with the armor, the armor seemed to melt, allowing Usato-kun's attacks through.

"The black knight's armor reflects any damage it takes, but it can't reflect Usato-kun's attacks because he's healing his attacks *before* they can be reflected."

All that remained, then, was Usato-kun's fists. His kicks and palm strikes. This was above and beyond simply hitting and being hurt. I couldn't help but laugh. It was outrageous. Unbelievable.

"That is *not* how you're supposed to use healing magic," I muttered.

Even if you could *use healing magic, who would even think to use it when attacking? And since when did healers run around beating people up, anyway?*

The answer, of course, was they didn't.

Just then, the black knight let out an enraged, frenzied cry at the one-sided barrage, raising her sword up high and wrapping it in her black armor.

"Wha?!" sputtered Usato-kun.

"You . . . You . . . I'll kill yoooou!!"

The black knight's eyes, visible through part of her helmet, were empty. She'd lost the grip on her own sanity. Her armor crawled and writhed in response to her shout, flowing to her sword. It wrapped around the blade, transforming it into a huge great sword. Usato-kun seemed to sense the danger and leaped back to where I was.

"U-Usato-kun?!"

"No need to worry. I'll finish her here and now."

"Finish her?!"

I couldn't believe what I was hearing, but Usato-kun stared straight ahead at the black knight, swinging her sword. She'd lost sight of everything but him. She swung her sword recklessly, wildly, prepared to destroy everything and anything in her path.

"I don't know what magic she uses and I don't care," said Usato-kun. "My job is still the same: make sure she can't hurt anyone else and help the fallen knights."

He clenched his fist tight, pouring his magic into it. It was just like the first time I saw it: a beautiful and warm healing light. He dashed toward the knight, his right fist held back and emanating a green glow.

"Usato-kun!"

I called his name before I even realized. But he was beyond my worry and my fears, picking up speed with each step he took. The light of the healing magic trailed behind him like a green comet. Usato-kun had worked hard to make the most of the two things he'd come to this world with—his physical abilities and his healing magic. Not even the black knight's sword could stand in his way.

Which was why Usato-kun's fist slammed into the black knight's stomach. She heaved at the impact of the strike. Perhaps due to the overwhelming amount of magic, her body glowed green through the gaps in her black armor for a brief instant. But one thing was clear: the strike had knocked her out cold. She collapsed and Usato-kun quickly tied her up in his Rescue Team coat.

"Talk about a sudden death round . . . Or, uh . . . sudden *life*, I guess?" muttered Usato-kun, hefting the black knight onto his shoulder. "Well, whatever. At least the healing punch finished the job."

All I could do was watch, perplexed, my head tilted in confusion.

With the black knight tied up and out of action, Usato-kun ran over to me and began healing the knights I'd been keeping alive with first aid magic.

He's so quick. Just like when he healed my wounds. Real healing magic is on a whole other level.

"What's a healing punch?" I asked as I watched the color return to the knights' faces. "You've got me totally stumped."

Usato-kun looked suddenly awkward.

"Oh," he said. "You, uh . . . you heard that?"

Why does he suddenly look like I'm the last person he wants to explain it to?!

"It's just wrapping my fist in healing magic. That's it. The captain taught me."

"Rose?"

"Yep. She said that if your aim is just to knock someone out, then you heal 'em as you hit 'em. I'm kind of a coward, you know? I don't want to hurt anyone, so it sounded like a good idea to me."

"Hm? Huh? Wait, Usato-kun. I think you've got things mixed up."

So the logic is: you hit them to hurt them, but then you heal them, and because you heal them, it's okay? That doesn't make sense. In the end, you're still hitting them!

Usato looked perplexed at my own confusion.

"Hm? Is something wrong? I mean, all her injuries are healed. She went unconscious because of the shock and the pain, but now she's not a problem, and I didn't even leave a bruise. I've actually already used this attack a few times to keep enemies off of me, and it feels pretty great."

Usato-kun, someone *has had a really legit bad influence on you.*

Then again, there's something crazy and insane about this world that's having that same influence on all of us.

"Hm . . ."

If not for the way the black knight's armor reacted to Usato-kun's healing punch, we would have been goners. That much is certain.

"You're so reliable, Usato-kun."

"Nah, I don't deserve that kind of praise. But more importantly, what are we going to do about the black knight?" asked Usato-kun, pointing to the girl on his shoulders as he stood. "I can't just stay here with her for the rest of the battle."

"She'll be taken as a prisoner, I imagine."

"They won't torture her or anything like that, will they?"

I kind of feel like someone *already tortured her, to be honest.*

But I didn't think that was what Usato-kun was getting at.

"King Lloyd doesn't seem like the type," I said. "I'm sure they'll only go as far as interrogating her."

Lloyd was such a kind ruler. I just couldn't imagine him being cruel.

But there was *one* thing that kept bothering me.

"How long are you going to stand there carrying the black kni . . . I mean *her* on your shoulder?"

Isn't it fine just to put her on the ground? No? You'll make a girl a little jealous. You'll make me *jealous.*

Usato-kun looked a little sheepish as he glanced at the black knight.

"My Rescue Team uniform acts as a kind of beacon. It lets knights know where the Rescue Team members are. So I can't just leave her lying around," he explained.

"I see. Then we'll have the knights bring a rope or something. And also . . ." I began.

"And also?"

"Thanks. You saved us. If you hadn't come when you did, we'd all be dead," I concluded.

That wound of mine was fatal.

It hurt like nothing I'd ever known.

I'll never forget the feeling of my blood leaking, draining from my body like that. I remember the words of regret that ran through my head: Is this where it ends? To die without even leaving a mark, to die having achieved nothing. To die as I let my friends and brothers in arms die around me.

It was the overwhelming pain of having given it my best, only to be left unable to keep my promise to protect the kingdom—the place we now called home.

Those thoughts crowded my brain, drowning me, and then . . . you came.

And I couldn't have been happier.

You saved us, just like you told me you would when we were at the training grounds. That made me so, so happy.

"Of course I came," Usato-kun said with a relieved smile. "You're my senpai, and Kazuki is my friend."

I nodded.

"But anyway, it looks like the enemy forces are retreating, senpai. Might be because we took down the black knight. One more push by the Llinger forces and the battle will swing in our favor."

Guess I'll have to save my gushing for later.

Usato-kun was right—our forces were fighting back, and with Siglis leading them, we had a real fighting chance.

"Suzune-sama! Kazuki-sama is awake!" cried a nearby knight.

Usato-kun and I rushed over to Kazuki-kun. It seemed he'd heard the details of the battle from the knight by his side, and he flashed us a smile as he rubbed at his stomach, where he'd been wounded.

"Are you okay, Kazuki?" asked Usato-kun.

Kazuki-kun laughed.

"Looks like you made it just in time. Thanks. You saved my life."

"I'm so sorry," I said. "This never would have happened if I hadn't been so reckless."

"Don't apologize. We didn't have much of a choice against that black knight," Kazuki responded.

Kazuki-kun stood to his feet and sheathed his sword. He gave his cheeks a slap as if he were waking himself up after a nap.

"Alright!" he said. "We've got a battle to fight, senpai! Let's go help the knights at the front lines!"

There was no point in asking him if he was sure he was okay—my own wounds were just as healed as his were. And we both had Usato-kun to thank for that. He'd brought us back from the literal brink of death.

Hm . . .

"Usato-kun, my life is now in your—"

"Save the small talk for later, yeah?"

I swallowed my words and looked out at the battlefield. The Llinger forces were fighting back and pushing the Demon Lord's army back. It wouldn't be easy, but if we could keep up the pressure, we had a real chance of achieving victory here.

"Let's hit them hard before they can regroup," I said. "Kazuki-kun, are you ready?"

"Good to go!"

"I'll head to the front lines just as soon as I make sure the black knight is properly bound," added Usato-kun.

"In that case, it looks like this is where we'll part ways for a time," said Kazuki-kun.

Usato-kun was as important to this battle as we were, though for different reasons. He couldn't afford to stay here for the entire battle with the black knight bound in his coat. A knight delivered him the rope we'd asked for and he quickly tied up the black knight's arms and legs.

But it was kind of, well . . .

"I'm getting kind of—no. I'm getting *strong* sinful and indecent vibes from this," I said.

"I told you already," said Usato-kun, "I'm *not* into that kind of thing!"

Now that the black knight wasn't going to be an issue, Usato-kun took back his coat and gave it a shake to make sure it wasn't ripped or torn anywhere. It looked like it had some weight to it.

"Well, that takes care of that, then," he said as he put his coat back on.

"Sir Usato, what should we do with her?" asked a knight.

"I don't have the authority to decide, so we'll have to leave that to Commander Siglis. Can I ask you to watch over her until he has a chance to make a decision? I'll be needed on the front lines."

"Yes, sir!" replied the knight, nothing if not conscientious.

Usato-kun nodded, feeling a bit awkward at the interaction, but by the time he turned back to face Kazuki-kun and me, he had his game face on.

"Senpai, Kazuki," he said. "Please don't put yourself in danger like that again. My healing magic is not all-powerful. Even I can't raise the dead."

"Got it. We'll try not to push it. You look out for yourself too, okay?" I told him.

Usato-kun looked relieved at my reply. Then he turned away from us and got ready to dash back out and into battle. Kazuki-kun and I were readying ourselves to do the same.

"Good luck out there, Usato-kun," I whispered.

But as I turned back to the knights awaiting my orders—

"Hang on a minute," said a voice.

"Hurk?!" squealed Usato-kun.

In the next instant, a beautiful green-haired woman appeared, gripping Usato-kun by the collar of his coat and stopping him before he could go anywhere at all.

* * *

She came out of nowhere. She had the glare of a monster, an oppressive, overwhelming aura, and a ferocious attitude hidden beneath her stunningly beautiful features.

Yes, she is the most frightening, most wicked—

"What is the meaning of this? Explain yourself, Usato," Rose barked.

"I-I-I-I-I will explain everything. Just let me go, Captain!"

She was my teacher, my superior, and the captain of the Rescue Team. Rose. And she looked down at me with a slight annoyance in her eyes.

"Well then, what happened?"

"Uh, well . . ."

I stammered my way through an explanation of recent events. At the end of it, Rose crossed her arms in thought.

Oh man, what do I do? She's terrifying. She's going to smack my head off my shoulders, I just know it . . . or maybe she'll settle for throwing me smack bang right in the middle of the Demon Lord's forces.

"I'd heard the heroes were in trouble. That's why I'm here. Surprised you handled everything already though."

"Sorry."

"No. No apology necessary. You did good."

"So what should I do now, Captain?"

I had a feeling I'd be heading back into battle but decided it best to ask Rose first.

"What indeed . . ." said Rose, glancing at Inukami-senpai and the knights with her. "The heroes are back in action, we've captured one of the enemy's key warriors, and now their forces are in disarray. Perfect."

"Right," I stated.

"We're heading back to camp," she said.

"What?!" I exclaimed.

I couldn't understand it. She wanted us to *retreat*?! If she was ordering me to return to Ururu and the others at the Rescue Team camp, did that mean I wasn't necessary on the front lines anymore?

"We're not needed here anymore," said Rose. "The battle is swinging in our favor. Unless the enemy forces have some hidden ace up their sleeve, we'll be fine. From this point, we'll only get in the knights' way."

"So it's best if we do our healing back at camp?"

"Exactly."

That makes sense. I'll head back with Rose then.

Even if I retreated, there was still a lot left for me to do. A part of me felt relieved to not have to run through the bloodbath of the battlefield, but the rest of me worried about senpai and Kazuki. Yes, they were covered in blood, but they both looked ready for action—they'd healed up nicely. That at least made me feel better.

"Kazuki, Inukami-senpai," I said. "I'm heading back to camp, but no dying out there for either of you. You're heroes. You smash those demons and you come back safe, okay?"

"You got it. I fully intend to treasure the life you saved," said senpai.

"Look after yourself, Usato," added Kazuki.

There was a weight to the words senpai spoke. I smiled in reply to both her and Kazuki, then left them with the knights and ran back to the rearguard with Rose. She muttered something under her breath as she sped off, but it was lost in cries that rang out through the battlefield.

I think she might have said, "Glad you made it out of that in one piece."

* * *

"WHAT?! What do you mean the black knight was captured?!"

The Demon Lord's main squad had gone to meet Llinger's

heroes head-on, and now the news came that the black knight had been defeated. Amila Vergrett, commander of the Demon Lord's third army, fell off her chair.

She couldn't believe it. The black knight's abilities were famous among the Demon Lord's forces. Not only could its armor defend and counter with ease, but the black knight could also transform the armor into weapons. Amila herself, who was exceptionally powerful, matched up badly with the knight, whose rare magic type always kept her on the defensive.

"Was it the heroes?!" she demanded.

"No, based on the white uniform, we believe it was a member of the Rescue Team. They appeared in our last battle," Hyriluk explained.

The image of a particular healer appeared in Amila's mind.

"White uniform . . . Was it Rose, then?!"

The woman could heal almost any injury in the blink of an eye. Capturing the black knight was perhaps not too difficult for one such as her.

"The soldiers say it wasn't Rose. They say it was a young boy with black hair."

The reply was *not* what Amila wanted to hear.

"There's another one? Shit."

What a nightmare. It was bad enough on the front lines with just Rose rushing around healing the Llinger forces, but now there was someone else to deal with?

And they captured the black knight?

It was like having two Roses on the battlefield.

Everyone believed in the overwhelming power of the black knight's strength. With the knight captured, the morale of the demon army would take a huge hit.

"Hyriluk. Call Baljinuk back," Amila barked.

Hyriluk was controlling Baljinuk from a distance via a magical seal.

"Are you certain?" he asked, shooting Amila a dubious glance.

Amila was going to take the best option available, though it vexed her to do so.

"Perhaps it would be best if I was out there, but as it stands, we won't be able to defend our base with just our soldiers. Commander Siglis still hasn't stepped foot on the battlefield either. It is pointless to keep fighting," she lamented.

"Indeed. We don't have the luxury of healing magic, which means there's nothing we can do to aid our fallen," Hyriluk noted.

Healing magic was a magic type unique to humans. Because the magical properties that allowed for magic differed between the two races, there were no demons capable of using healing magic. It was unknown exactly why, but it was a vexing reality for the demons.

"I will take full responsibility," said Amila. "Your snake will be put to better use in our next battle, Hyriluk. At present, it will only impede the retreat of our soldiers. Call it back."

"Understood. You're making the right decision. The humans were simply stronger this time. Hm?!"

"What is it?"

"It's the heroes . . ."

Hyriluk held his head in his hands. Through the magical seal in front of him, which showed what the snake Baljinuk could see, there appeared the two heroes standing side by side.

* * *

In front of us was a giant snake. A monster. The knights' attacks had been entirely futile. This was unlike any snake we had ever known, and it hissed poison gas as it curled up in wait. But I was strangely unafraid.

"The enemy soldiers are retreating," I said.

"A little more and it's all over, then?" Kazuki-kun asked.

"I sure hope so."

I stared ahead toward the snake, which glared back at us. It bared its huge fangs and let out a guttural roar in an attempt to intimidate us.

"Looks like the snake is still raring to go," I said.

"Senpai, we can't allow it to harm anyone else."

"I know. That's why we're taking it down."

I took my sword from its scabbard and cast my own magic. Electricity flowed from my hand into the blade of my sword, imbuing it with a golden light. Kazuki-kun did likewise, sending light magic into his sword while also gathering it in his free hand until he had a sphere of light and a blade ready to dispel evil.

"No more humiliating ourselves in battle," I said.

"Just like Usato said: smash the demons and go home safe," said Kazuki-kun.

Surrounded by light and thunder, Kazuki-kun and I clenched our swords tight and dashed toward the snake. It was a fearsome enemy, but it would not stand in our way. Not now. We had something to fight for. We had a friend awaiting our return, and we had people to protect—people who had kindly welcomed us into the world they called home.

This was why I wielded my blade!

* * *

I saw a light flashing on the front lines of battle and the figure of a giant snake.

It looked not unlike the giant snake I'd encountered in the forest. But I didn't need to worry about senpai and Kazuki, who were fighting it.

I didn't need to worry because they were heroes.

If it struggled with the likes of me, it didn't stand a chance against them.

"Usato! Ya better not be slacking off!" shouted Tong as he carried another injured knight into the tent.

"Shut your trap! I'm no slacker!" I shouted back, laying the knight down on the hemp mats lining the ground.

The tent was packed, so I got to work healing the wounded knight immediately.

"Ngh, hah . . ." he muttered.

"Are you okay?" I said, putting a hand to the muscly knight's shoulder, where he was injured. I could tell by his complexion that it was poison, probably from the snake out there on the battlefield. Ordinary first aid magic wouldn't heal him, but my healing magic could. I closed the wound quickly, then put my hands to his shoulder and ribs and sent healing magic rushing through him.

"I'm getting kind of tired," I said with a sigh.

Come to think of it, I'd been running nonstop. And yeah, it was to help those fighting on the front lines, but it sure was a lot of footwork. If the old me could see me now, he probably wouldn't believe it.

"Ugh, uh . . ." muttered the knight.

He was regaining consciousness now that the poison in his blood was starting to fade. I knew he'd be fine, so I turned my attention to whom to help next.

"Y-You're on the Rescue Team," the knight said as I stood to my feet. "You saved me. Thank you."

"I'm just happy you're still alive," I said. "Please rest a little longer. You'll need a little time before you can start moving again."

I looked around for someone to heal. There were so many from the main force. Looking at them all made me uncomfortable—I didn't like seeing so many hurt and in pain.

A huge bolt of lightning and a pillar of light shone from the front lines of the battle. As they dissipated, I saw the snake, now burned as black as charcoal. It collapsed on its side.

"Looks like they did it," muttered Rose, who must have walked up to me while I was watching.

"Looks like it," I agreed.

The snake had been keeping the Demon Lord's army together, but its fall shook them into disarray, and the remaining soldiers ran for the border where the river ran through the plains.

"We're not going after them?" I asked.

"Idiot," said Rose. "Even if we've won this battle, we're still lacking in backup support. There's no need to drag the battle out and make any unnecessary sacrifices. We're better off preparing for the next one."

"So . . . they'll be back."

Rose said nothing in reply, only nodded. Then she knelt down and put a palm to the wounds of a knight who was just then brought to the tent. I was about to tell her that I would take over and do it for her, but she stopped me with a hand.

"By saving the heroes in this battle, you paved the way to victory for us," she said.

"But if I hadn't gotten to them, you still would have. Either way, they would have been saved."

"No. If you hadn't gotten to them, they would have died."

Rose finished healing the knight in seconds, then ran a hand through her hair and looked at me.

"You saved them," she said. "Not Siglis and not me. We were able to end this battle quickly because of you. If we'd screwed up, the heroes would be dead, and the battle could well have been lost."

Rose stood to her feet, her gaze firmly on my own.

"You did good, Usato. You did exactly as a Rescue Team member should."

Wow, so even Rose is capable of praising people. But what is this? I'm kind of . . . no, I'm **really** *happy. I don't know if it makes up for the hell that I went through to get here, but I feel like all my hard work was worth it.*

I was summoned to another world.

Taken away by Rose.

Made friends with a thuggish-looking gang.

Got thrown into a hellscape of a training routine.

Then got thrown into a forest.

Chased bears and met Blurin.

Fought a snake and almost died.

Drifted into the forest with Inukami-senpai.

Met Orga and Ururu.

And then, when the real battle started . . .

"Huh?" I muttered.

My cheeks were wet. I didn't want to cry, but the tears refused to stop. I wiped at them with my sleeve, but they just kept flowing from me.

I felt something cover my head. Rose had put the hood of my uniform over me.

"So you do have a childish side in there," she said.

"Of course," I said. "I'm seventeen."

I realized then that when I first came to this place, I was anxious and scared. Everything happened so fast that I didn't even have a chance to know how I felt. Rose's words seemed to break the dam of emotions inside of me.

"It's so terrifying out there on the battlefield," I said. "The demons too. I saw so many out there, just dying. It was so, so hard."

But I had also made important connections. With Inukami-senpai and Kazuki. With the king and everyone at the castle. With Rose and her idiot crew, and with Ururu and Orga. Since I came here, those ties had brought me happiness. I was just a boring kid in my old world—I didn't deserve these blessings.

As magic launched to signal the end of the battle, I looked once more at Rose.

"I'm glad I met you, and I'm so glad I could help," I told her.

Rose's eyes grew wide with surprise, but then she shot me a wry grin, and there was kindness in her eyes.

"In the past, there were others who said that same thing to me. They're little more than memories now, but you are still here. You did good, Usato. You came back."

"Thank you!" I replied through the tears.

But I realized then that I'd hit my limit. My legs wobbled underneath me. I just couldn't get them to listen to me. As my consciousness began to fade, I felt Rose grab me by the waist and heft me onto her shoulder.

"Huh?" I muttered.

"All out of magic, and all out of stamina," she said. "You did the best you could. Rest now because you're in for a heck of a time when you wake up."

Rose smiled at something that was very amusing to her, but I didn't have much time to think about it as I slipped into unconsciousness.

CHAPTER 3

New Beginnings!

We had earned victory over the Demon Lord's army. And though the Llinger forces had suffered their fair share of casualties, I was glad at least that so many had survived. The work of the Rescue Team had not been in vain; I could say that much for certain.

However, there had still been much to do after I passed out, and it hadn't been easy. The wounded who could not move on their own had to be helped, discarded weapons had to be gathered so they could not be put to nefarious use, and a host of other similar tasks had to be seen to once the battle was over.

Tong told me all of this—complained about it, really—after I woke from a three-day slumber, so it must have been tough work. Putting aside Tong himself and his fellow meatheads, Orga and Ururu weren't particularly physically strong, so I was really glad to hear that the Rescue Team members were all okay.

The day after I awoke, Inukami-senpai and Kazuki received medals of valor from the king, which were awarded in front of the kingdom's citizens. I was clapping and thinking about how amazing it was when Rose and I were called up to the king too.

Huh? Why me?

I was all sorts of confused, but Rose had this wicked grin on her face, and she slapped me on the back and forced me up toward the king. When I reached him, the citizens—mostly the knights—let out a tremendous cheer. I decided the best approach was to bow my way through it all in typical Japanese fashion until Rose punched me, and then I hobbled over and received a medal of honor for valiant work in the field.

When I asked what I'd done, I was told the medal represented my contribution to our victory: the many lives saved, and the successful capture of an enemy captain.

"Take it," said Rose. "It's an honor."

Her words made me tremble inside.

"It was this whole royal ordeal, Blurin," I said. "Nothing like I'm used to."

Blurin growled in response.

After that, I'd spent the next week living pretty much the way I was used to, and that brought me to Blurin's stable, where I told him all about the last battle. Blue Grizzlies were known for their intelligence, and it was said that with work, they could even understand human language. With that in mind, I took it upon myself to talk to Blurin often. Unfortunately, the grizzly only let out a long yawn like a cow mooing; he showed exactly zero interest in my story.

"I really should have brought you with me," I said. "And speaking of which, you've gotta get some exercise. Too much loafing and you'll forget your wild roots."

I slapped the bear lightly on the head until he stood to his feet. I usually carried Blurin on my back, but I figured it was good sometimes to make him walk on his own. I'd also been summoned by the king, so I thought I'd take Blurin along with me for the walk. He was getting bigger little by little, but if he only ever got fatter, he'd end up just a useless glutton.

"Let's go, Blurin," I said.

The grizzly growled a lazy response and walked alongside me. I chuckled at the sight of him lumbering along—just another fun part of our everyday life. We were in high spirits as we headed out, and then I noticed a figure running toward us from the Rescue Team's living quarters.

"Usato-kun!"

Ururu ran toward us with a wave. She was a healer, like me, and about the same age too.

"Hey, Ururu," I said.

"How are you feeling?"

"Great," I said. "Slept like a rock."

"Good to hear! I was so worried about you and Rose, out there on the front lines of the battle . . . Oh! Hello there, Blurin!"

Ururu gave Blurin a little wave, but the bear simply turned his nose up at her and looked away. The gesture clearly stung, but she pulled herself together even as she looked back at me with a twitchy smile.

"Y-You're going for a walk?"

"No, I was summoned by the king. But I also thought I'd make sure Blurin got a little exercise."

Ururu laughed.

"I see," she said. "Well, if you're going into town, do be careful."

"Careful? Careful of what?"

"Well, I shouldn't leave my brother waiting, so I better get going!"

Weird. It's like she didn't want me asking her anything more.

Is something going on in town? Maybe the townsfolk are angry about all the people I couldn't save?

Those who were lost in battle had been buried in the kingdom's cemetery. I'd been there for the funerals, and I could imagine some people were upset. If they told me that I wasn't strong enough, or that I didn't do enough, I couldn't deny it.

If the people of the kingdom were angry or upset, then I would have to accept it and take it on the chin.

Blurin and I reached the castle gates without issue. The gates were surrounded by the castle walls and its moat and guarded by two knights in heavy armor. One of them, the one with red hair, was the gatekeeper, Aruku. As soon as he saw me, he ran over with a huge smile.

"Sir Usato! How are you feeling?"

"All good. I'm glad to see that you look well too." I remembered then that Aruku had watched over and protected Orga and Ururu. "Thanks again for looking after all of us in the battle."

"No, no! It's our job to defend the Rescue Team. All of you are essential and irreplaceable! If anyone should be saying thanks, it should be us knights thanking the Rescue Team!"

Aruku bowed deeply. The knight behind him took off his helmet and followed suit. I was shocked by the sudden gesture. Aruku spoke again, his head still bowed.

"Because of you and Madam Rose, I—no, *we*—made it back home safely."

"But there were still so many I couldn't save," I said.

"Be that as it may, without your efforts, many more never would have made it home."

"Oh, but . . . Er . . . Look, please. Raise your heads."

I wasn't used to being praised like this. It wasn't that I wasn't glad for it, but I felt flustered in the face of such earnest gratitude. Blurin yawned as I patted him on the head and looked for the right words.

"I couldn't have done it on my own," I said. "There were many times in that battle that I thought I was a goner, but I was saved by the knights. We won this battle together."

Aruku was momentarily stunned by my words but then chuckled and scratched his head.

"I see. You really are an interesting one, Sir Usato . . . Oh! You must have business at the castle if you've come all this way. We'll open the gates immediately!"

"Yeah, business . . . something like that, I think . . ."

The knights sprang into action when they remembered why I was there. I thanked them. Then Blurin and I walked through the gates into the huge grounds of the royal kingdom.

Man, it never ceases to amaze me how huge this place is.

I walked along stone-brick paths leading away from the guards to the entrance to the castle. I left Blurin outside. I knew he'd be fine—he was a peaceful sort at heart.

After I entered the castle proper, a maid took me to the king. Along the way, the knights we passed showered me with praise just like Aruku had at the gates. The maid and I eventually arrived at a hall where the kindly king was waiting together with Sergio and Commander Siglis.

"Hello there, Usato," said the king.

"Your Majesty," I replied.

"I apologize for calling you here so suddenly."

"It's no problem whatsoever," I said. "Um . . . May I ask *why* you called me?"

"Yes, about that . . ." said the king, casting a gaze at the commander. "Siglis."

"Sire!" said Siglis, taking a step forward. "Usato-sama, do you remember the enemy you captured?"

"Yes . . ."

He was talking about the black knight, a wielder of heretical dark magic. She had pushed Inukami-senpai and Kazuki to the literal brink of death. After the battle was over, I found out that the only reason I'd been able to take her down was that my healing magic canceled out her own magic, rendering her armor useless against my punches and kicks. But when I thought more about it, I realized that only Rose or I could have handled the black knight—Ururu and Orga just weren't able to do it through physical power.

But why are they asking **me** *about the black knight?*

Wait, no way—

"She didn't . . . kill herself, did she?"

It was certainly a plausible scenario. I'd heard of cases where people taken as prisoners of war feared horrid torture and so chose to take their own lives. I was certain that Llinger Kingdom wouldn't resort to torture, but still, it was possible the black knight hadn't wanted to find out.

"She did not. To be honest, she's been surprisingly responsive to our interrogations."

"Huh?"

"I know it must come as a surprise," said Siglis, placing a hand to his forehead. "It certainly was for me to see it with my own eyes."

But if she's so easy to interrogate, why summon me?

"It would seem the black knight isn't particularly loyal to the Demon Lord's army," said Siglis. "She's already given us some very useful intel, though she did so somewhat reluctantly."

"And it's not a trap?" I asked.

"Of course, we must take what she says with a grain of salt, but it is useful to consider all the same."

That only made sense. The moment she went along with the interrogation would have been cause for concern and suspicion. But even after considering Siglis's words, I still couldn't work out why I was there.

"So why did you need to summon me?" I asked.

"She insists on meeting you, Usato-sama."

"WHAT?"

"That's why we summoned you," said the king. "To arrange a meeting with the black knight."

"Huh? But, your Majesty, all I did was capture her!"

"You make it sound like it was but a simple task. The black knight easily overpowered our two heroes. Outside of yourself and Rose, nobody in the kingdom would stand a chance."

"Er . . ."

The king's words left me confused. If anything, the black knight held nothing but enmity for me. And now I had to go and meet her?

I don't know if I have the guts for this.

"The black knight has said she will provide us with valuable intelligence if we can meet her one condition: a meeting with you, Usato-sama."

I thought I was free from all the fighting for a while . . . Now I'm stuck in the middle of a whole other mess.

"Has she said what that valuable intelligence is?" I asked.

I had to ask. It was a major responsibility they were asking of me.

"Of course," said the king. "She has agreed to tell us the magic types of the commanders of the Demon Lord's second and third armies, along with their powers."

Damn. That's not just valuable. It's practically priceless.

* * *

The sound of footsteps echoed as we walked down to the basement. I was accompanied by Commander Siglis himself and his most trusted guard. I felt in safe hands.

Except for one thing . . .

"Rest easy, Usato-kun! At the very least, I can be a shield for you!"

For some reason, Inukami-senpai was also tagging along.

"Look, I'm glad you're aware you don't stand a chance, but I'm not so big on the pessimistic attitude . . ."

Don't get me wrong, I was happy she was worried about me, but to be honest, I was pretty certain she was only going to make things more complicated. Meanwhile, Kazuki was somewhere with Celia. That guy was really making the most of things here. But it made sense that someone like him got to live the good life. I really hoped he was enjoying it.

"Well, the only ones who can stand up to the black knight are you and Rose. A shield is the best I can do right now."

"Healing magic isn't supposed to be for hurting people though."

Even when I was fighting the black knight, all I wanted was to render her unconscious.

Wait a second. My healing magic canceled out the black knight's magic, right? That meant she just ate my punches raw, because the two magics nullified each other.

What if she's actually badly injured?

I beat the crap out of her because I thought my healing magic was working the whole time.

"Siglis! Did you use any first aid on the black knight?" I asked.

"No, she's been in her armor the whole time. Is something the matter? Is she wounded? She certainly didn't look as if she was injured."

"Usato-kun . . ." said Inukami-senpai. She realized what I was thinking, and her face grew pale.

"This is bad," I muttered.

Every attack I'd thrown at the black knight had landed flush. No defenses. And not to brag, but I could break rocks with my punches without breaking a sweat. Inukami-senpai and I took off down the stairs and deeper into the basement.

At the bottom of the stairs was a guard. Behind him, the black knight was crouched in the corner of her cell.

"Sir Usato!" said the guard. "Is something wrong?!"

"Usato?" said the black knight, raising her head at the guard's voice. She stood up, looking at us. I smelled traces of blood in the air.

Does she have injuries from the battle?

I didn't know why, but I just knew I had to help her.

"We meet again, healer," said the black knight.

"You're hurt, aren't you?" I replied.

"I am. But it doesn't matter," said the black knight, her voice difficult to hear through her helmet. "So this is what you call pain, huh?"

I heard something not unlike childish joy in her voice. Inukami-senpai heard it, too, and grabbed the sleeve of my coat.

"Usato-kun, she's fascinating. She's a total masochist and she doesn't even know it. But it looks like she's not nearly at my level when it comes to personality."

"Could you please shut up for a second?"

Also, it's not like the two of you are in some competition.

I took a deep breath and faced the black knight again.

"Why did you want to see me?" I asked.

"I wanted to see the man responsible for putting me here," she said, then flinched and chuckled. "Ow, that kind of stings. It hurts to move."

The black knight put a hand to her side and wobbled on her feet.

Ugh, she's just like Inukami-senpai. They're both twisted.

"Pass me the key, please," I said to the guard.

"Are you sure, Sir Usato?"

"Usato-kun?!" said Inukami-senpai.

As a member of the Rescue Team, I could not stand by and do nothing when I saw somebody in pain. Inukami-senpai's face flinched as she tried to hold me back, but she simply wasn't strong enough. I shrugged her off and walked toward the guard, just as Siglis arrived.

"What is the meaning of this?" he asked.

* * *

I watched the healer that was outside of my cage. The female hero tried to hold him back, and then a huge knight pointed at me and shouted something with one heck of a stern look on his face.

Whatever. It had nothing to do with me. I ignored them. I felt that strange sensation assault my body again. I sighed as it pulsed in my stomach.

What is this strange sensation?

As a demon, I was both resilient and quick to heal. But even with that, and even though I had my impenetrable armor protecting me, I had still gotten hurt. I'd never been hurt like this. Not ever. I guessed this was what people called "being in severe pain."

I touched the parts of me that ached and I turned my gaze once more on the healer.

Healing magic. It was a rare magic that only appeared in humans. Its power was as simple and straightforward as its name suggested. I had heard by listening to my guards that this particular healer was Rose's student. She was the one the third army commander was so concerned about.

I had always looked down on healers, and for that, I had paid a tremendous price. Who would have thought it would break through my dark magic?

It was you. You're the one who hurt me.

The one who gave me this pain. This defeat.

I—

"I'm coming inside."

The cage door opened with a clank as the healer stepped into my cell.

"What now? Torture?" I asked.

"Put out your hand."

"Huh? Why?"

"I said **put out your hand**!"

"Eep!"

My hand was out before I realized it.

So the Llinger Kingdom's healers have learned to utilize the power of a murderous glare, then.

In that single instant, the calm, merciful look on the healer's face had morphed into that of a monster. I was used to being berated and shouted at, but *this* was a moment of true fear.

"Why would they just leave you like this?" he asked. "Oh, wait. I'm the one who did it, aren't I?"

The healer gently took my hand. His own lit up with the light of healing magic. I felt it wrap around my hand. My body accepted it through our connected hands.

"What are you doing?!" I demanded.

The warm light wrapped around my hand, then spread to my shoulder, my head, my chest, and my back.

"I'm healing you."

"I don't *need* your healing!"

I tried to shake him off, but his grip, though gentle, was like a vise. It wouldn't budge. The healer raised his other hand to my left cheek, where he'd hit me during our fight.

"I would feel utterly horrible if you were to die on me," he said. "I don't want that hanging over my head. So shut up and let me heal you."

The magic passed through my helmet and his hand touched my face. It was unbelievably warm. Until now, I hadn't let anyone touch me, not even my parents. But for some reason, I found myself placing my hand upon the healer's own.

"Usato-kun!" shouted the hero outside the cage.

"It's fine . . . probably," said the healer.

"Probably?!"

I didn't know how to express the feelings that welled inside of me. The healing light that enveloped me, the warm touch so different from a demon's—all of it was unknown to me, and yet I pined for it.

I let out a sigh as the hand on my cheek relaxed, and the healing magic surrounding me dissipated. The pain that once wracked my body was gone within seconds.

And yet I did not release my grip upon the healer's hand. A suspicious expression grew upon the face of the healer.

"Uh, maybe let go of me, please?" he asked. "I'm kind of scared now."

"Just a little longer . . ."

"Huh?"

"Touch me, please, just a little longer."

His hand, touching my cheek. It's wet.

No, not his hand. My other cheek is wet too.

I didn't understand. I reached up and touched my cheek, my helmet disappearing as I did so. The healer let out an exasperated sigh.

"How am I supposed to say no when you go crying on me like that?"

Ah, that's what it is. I'm crying.

Through my wavering gaze, I saw the awkward look upon the face of the healer, and I felt that I was seeing a "human" for the first time. I had seen him and everyone in this world as pointless. Without value. But warmth now bloomed at the bottom of my heart.

It would not be long before I understood that sensation to be kindness. I no longer cared if the person in front of me was friend or foe. It didn't matter—I just did not want to let go of the feeling.

And so I clung to the hand at my cheek with everything I had.

* * *

The black knight—or, more accurately, the silver-haired girl—gave us the intelligence she promised. I don't know if she was satisfied at having finally spoken to me, but I was at least glad that I could help out.

Once I finished reporting to the king, I left the castle. For some reason, Inukami-senpai decided to tag along.

Doesn't she have anything better to do?

Just as I was thinking this and other similar thoughts, Inukami-senpai turned to me. A smile rose to her face.

"A new challenger appears, and one from among the enemy, no less. Guess I shouldn't expect anything less from the man I've got my eyes on!"

"Do you always have to talk so crazy?"

I don't know where or how you saw a challenger in any of that.

I mean, we're talking about the same black knight, right?

"All I did was my job," I said. "And besides, girls don't go for guys like me anyway."

"You can't say that!"

"And why not?"

"Is there not a challenger standing right in front of your eyes?!"

A moment of silence passed between the two of us.

"Anyway, I know she's the enemy and all," I said, "but I think I might have gone a little too far in that last battle."

"Wait. Did you just ignore me?"

The answer was yes. I did what I could to ignore senpai and thought of the black knight. When I'd first seen her on the battlefield, I'd thought she was young, but I'd never thought we'd be around the same age. Siglis and the knights were shocked to find there was a young girl inside that terrifying suit of armor.

"Just to be clear, you shouldn't just go touching a girl's face like that, even if it's for healing," said Inukami-senpai.

"But I mean . . . I literally punched her lights out, you know? I mean, to put it into perspective, it was comparable to flatlining that giant snake you and Kazuki fought."

"Oh, okay . . . I can sympathize with that."

There was no real getting around it on the battlefield, but now she was a prisoner. And now that she was answering our questions, it was getting harder to see her as an enemy. The last thing I wanted to do was beat on someone like that and just let them die.

Then again, when Inukami-senpai and Kazuki had been hurt, I just snapped.

"In that fight, I was just pure rage. I thought she'd killed you and Kazuki. I'm just so glad that the two of you are alive."

Senpai laughed.

"You really know how to make a friend happy when you talk like that," she said, patting me on the shoulder.

As we left the castle, I heard heavy stomps coming from the training grounds, and then a blue shape leaped at me with a gruff roar.

"Wha?!"

At the same time as I gasped in momentary shock, I caught the giant blue Blurin in my arms and placed him on the floor. Then we went on walking together.

Inukami-senpai was frozen in place, her jaw hanging low.

"Something wrong?" I asked.

"Wait, wait, wait, what?! Who wouldn't be surprised at a guy just catching a flying grizzly?!"

"Oh, that. I'm used to it, that's all. Are you coming to town or what?"

I was used to people being surprised by Blurin, so I didn't think anything of it. Blurin let out a little grumble.

"Sometimes I feel like I don't even know you anymore, Usato-kun," muttered Inukami-senpai.

For whatever reason, since the last battle, I'd felt odd. Fidgety. Like I couldn't sit still. So I started doing push-ups. But because it was the middle of the night, Rose chewed me out and kicked me as hard as she could. But I guess, all things considered, I was the one in the wrong for working out so late.

"But at least Blurin's still as cute as always!" I said.

Inukami reached out a hand to pet the grizzly but was met with a growl and a swift dodge out of the way.

Why won't he let her pat him? He's mostly okay with me doing it . . . Perhaps you have to gain his trust first?

"If you're heading out," I said, "perhaps it's better to wear a disguise."

"That goes for you too. To the people of this country—well, no, to *us*—you're a hero."

But even if I put my hood up, everyone would recognize me the moment they saw Blurin, so I decided not to worry about the disguise.

"So you're heading into town too, Usato-kun?" asked Inukami-senpai.

"Yep. I saw Ururu before heading to the castle, but I wanted to drop by and say hello to Orga too."

"You're both healers, after all," she said.

"Right. Orga is different to me. He's not physically strong, but his healing magic is levels above my own."

"Really . . ."

I'd heard that, just like me, Orga had collapsed at the end of the battle too. He'd woken up much sooner than I had, but all the same, I was still worried about him. I mean, I knew he'd be fine because he had Ururu, but I still wanted to drop by.

"Hm?"

"What's up?" asked senpai.

There was a girl with blonde hair at the entrance to town. In this world, there were all sorts of hair colors, so that on its own wasn't surprising. But the moment I saw it, the corners of my mouth curled into a grin. The girl was facing away from us, but I could still clearly see the triangular ears poking up from her head.

I took off after her immediately.

"Got you!" I shouted.

"Usato-kun?!" cried senpai.

I hit the ground so fast I covered the distance between us in seconds. The beastkin girl turned as if she was expecting me. I grabbed her under the arms and lifted her up into the air.

"You have some explaining to do!" I shouted.

This was the girl who had shown me the vision of Inukami-senpai and Kazuki being killed. Her eyes grew wide when she looked at my face. She mumbled for a time before she finally spoke, her voice clear.

"Healer, you're alive. In which case, you can return my favor."

"What?"

I heard senpai and Blurin catching up to me. I looked at the beastkin girl, who stared back at me, expressionless. As our eyes met, her face grew troubled.

"Please, save my mother," she said.

* * *

Save my mother.

That was what the beastkin girl asked of me.

The paying back of a favor, she called it. The favor, I guess, meant her showing me the vision that allowed me to save Inukami-senpai and Kazuki. And to be fair, if I'd never seen the vision, there was every chance that the heroes would have fallen, and Llinger Kingdom would have lost to the Demon Lord's army.

So I took the beastkin girl—along with Blurin and Inukami-senpai—back to the Rescue Team living quarters. At least at the quarters there was no chance of anyone around town overhearing our conversation. So if we discussed anything that needed to be kept secret, there was nowhere better.

After I took Blurin back to his stable, I sat the beastkin girl down at the food hall table, where Inukami-senpai and I sat across from her.

"Okay," I said. "Let's talk."

"Hey, Usato-kun, I don't have any idea what you guys have been talking about. And more importantly, who's this girl with the fox ears? She's adorable. Can I pet her?" Inukami-senpai asked.

"You're the only person I can rely on," said the girl.

"Me? Only me?" I asked.

"Am I invisible? Do you enjoy torturing me, Usato-kun? Well, that's fine. As long as I'm allowed to sit here enjoying this whole thing, that's exactly what I'm going to do," Inukami-senpai went on.

Just how much attention do you need, girl?

I gave the sulking Inukami-senpai a brief rundown of recent events, then thought about what the beastkin had just said. What did she mean that I was the only person she could rely on? If it was a healer she wanted, she could have easily gone to Orga or Ururu at their infirmary.

"I'm Amako," said the girl, introducing herself. "As you can see, I'm a fox beastkin. I know you already: you're the weird healer, Usato."

"Yeah, okay," I said, "so I'm well aware I haven't been using the power normally, but . . . whatever. There's so much I want to ask you. Firstly, why did you show me that premonition?"

The premonition was where it all started—the vision of Inukami-senpai and Kazuki dead. The girl was silent for a moment as she glanced worriedly at Inukami-senpai. Then she seemed to make up her mind. She turned back to me and started speaking.

"If I didn't, this kingdom would be done for. The heroes would have died, the kingdom would have fallen, and the country would be decimated—everything would be gone."

"What do you think?" I asked senpai.

"She might be right," she replied. "If you hadn't come when you did, Kazuki and I would be dead. And I don't mean to brag, but the Llinger forces would never have been able to push back the Demon Lord's army without us."

So things really had come right down to the wire.

Does that mean that I changed the kingdom's fate by doing what I did? I had been made a pivotal point of history and I didn't even know it. And if this beastkin hadn't shown me that premonition, the people of the kingdom, they'd all be . . .

My hands trembled just thinking about it.

"There are people here who look after me," said Amako, "and more than anything else, I couldn't lose you—not when I'd finally found you."

Finally found me?

Something about those words stuck in my mind.

"What exactly was it that you showed me? It wasn't an illusion, was it?"

Amako hesitated for a moment before speaking.

"I . . . my magic allows me to see the future," she said.

"Prescience, huh? I guess there's a magic for everything," I stated flatly.

I'd thought she had that kind of power, and her story proved it. Still, reading the future felt much more like a superpower than it did a magic type.

"I first saw the Llinger Kingdom fall in battle one year ago. So I started looking for a healer before the battle started. I was looking for someone who could heal any illness or injury."

"If you knew the kingdom was going to fall, why not leave?" asked senpai. "I know it's weird for me to ask, seeing as you saved my life, but wouldn't you have been better off running somewhere safer?"

"Senpai, the beastkin are often targeted outside of the kingdom," I said. "She probably couldn't leave even if she'd wanted to."

Amako nodded at my words.

"This was the only place that was safe," she said. "That is the extent to which the beastkin are persecuted."

It was very likely that this girl had been through terrifying ordeals just to get to the kingdom in the first place. Even if she could see the future, she was still a mostly powerless child otherwise.

"I came from the country of the beastkin," said Amako. "The Beastlands."

"That's . . . quite the distance," said Inukami-senpai.

"How far is it from the Llinger Kingdom?" I asked.

"Way too far for such a young child to travel alone."

Based on senpai's serious expression, I could tell it was no short distance.

"It wasn't hard on you?" I asked.

"I didn't think it so, because I focused on saving my mother."

"Your mother . . . is she sick?"

"They say she can't be healed normally. She won't wake up."

And so she needed a healer.

"Beastkin can't become healers. That magic is for humans only. But no matter where I went, there were no humans who could heal my mother. Nobody would help me because I'm a beastkin."

"Racial discrimination," muttered Inukami-senpai.

But I was thinking about something entirely different. Amako had been to a number of different countries in search of a healer. I had to imagine her magical powers of prescience helped her out of a few tight spots too. With such a powerful and convenient magic at her disposal, why would the beastkin even let her out of the country in the first place?

Amako went on.

"I found only three healers in this country, and I saw only two of them in futures where my mother and I were saved."

"And those three were Orga, Ururu, and the Rescue Team captain?"

"Yes. But when I got here, things didn't work out."

"How so?"

"The two people at the infirmary can't fight. The other one, the scary person, she listened to my story, but she wouldn't come with me."

"Oh . . ."

I could see that. Neither Ururu nor Orga had the strength and stamina for a long journey. Rose, on the other hand, was the leader of a small organization. She couldn't just pick up and leave whenever she wanted, though I could also picture her hearing the story and being like, "Yeah, right. What a cock-and-bull story."

"And that's where I come into the picture," I said.

"You're the one who could come with me. I knew it the moment I saw you. You could change the future of the kingdom and save my mother. That's why I showed you the vision."

"Is it easy for you to show other people the future?" I asked. "That was one heck of a headache."

It was so bad I thought my head was going to split open.

"It takes a lot of magic power for me to show people my visions. After I showed you, I slept for three days and three nights."

So that explained why I couldn't find her after the first vision. Still, she was responsible for saving senpai and Kazuki. And not just them, but the citizens of the kingdom too. I wanted to help her out, but this was getting to be a much bigger problem than I thought. According to Rose, the beastkin didn't take kindly to humans. And until we knew who this girl was to the Beastlands, I didn't want to do anything rash.

"Well, let's talk to the king, yeah?" I said. "We'll have to explain it to him, so will you come with me?"

"To see the king? Me?"

"I don't think he'll mind."

Of course, he was royalty—we'd need to make an appointment. I'd have to go through Rose to get it.

"Okay," I said. "Let's start with the Rescue Team captain. You can stay here with Inukami-senpai. And if she tries anything weird, you just shout for me, okay?"

"Usato-kun, really. Who do you think I am?" Inukami-senpai grumbled.

A girl who doesn't know how to sit still.

I glanced at senpai as I headed for the captain's office.

Rose is usually in her office around this time. The question is, how do I explain this to her?

* * *

Usato-kun looked a little worn out as he left the food hall. It was just me and the fox beastkin, Amako, who was sitting up nice and neatly in her chair. I rested my head on my hands and looked at her. She was fidgety and a little awkward.

. . .

And so cute.

So unbearably cute.

She's like a doll. I can't believe it.

She's a real live fox girl. She has the ears.

And the tail!

I wonder if she'll let me touch it.

Wait. Wait. Can't do that. Nope.

Almost lost my cool for a second there.

Phew.

First things first, let's summarize what she told us.

We knew that the girl had come from the Beastlands, and it had been anything but an easy journey. We also knew that her mother was sick, and she wanted Usato-kun to heal her. So she showed him a vision of the future in which I died and then he changed history and saved the kingdom from destruction. As repayment, she was calling in a favor.

The first thing I thought was how oddly roundabout the whole setup was.

"Couldn't you have just asked Usato-kun for his help? Why bring in the favor?" I asked.

"Before I came here, I would have. But then I met the Llinger people. That changed things."

"Ah, okay . . ."

The Llinger Kingdom, ruled over by King Lloyd, was almost perplexing in terms of its peacefulness. It was a unique nation where everyone was kind and discrimination didn't exist. Amako had probably come here expecting everyone to be her enemy and then found out that wasn't the case.

"This place is even kinder than my own hometown. Everyone treats each other as equals . . . but because my mother is in such pain . . . I need to take Usato to her."

The girl strung the words together little by little. She was missing the clarity she had when she spoke with Usato-kun . . . Probably she was still frightened of me.

This girl, she doesn't trust me yet.

"When I first saw Usato, I couldn't believe it," Amako said. "He didn't look like the kind of person who could save the kingdom from destruction."

"Just how does your magic work, anyway? There have to be limits to your ability to see the future, right?"

That said, I already knew it was powerful—Amako had

seen us lose the battle against the Demon Lord's army a whole year ago.

"It's very vague and unclear. I usually can't see more than the near future. But when I sleep, I can see further—sometimes half a year, sometimes a year. And for people who have the power to change it, I see two futures. And I can show the future only to the people who can choose a different path."

"So that's why you could show Usato us dying, and he could stop that from happening. Is prescience a common magic among the beastkin?"

"It's connected to my bloodline."

"Your bloodline?"

"My family is particularly skilled at reading the flow of time. My mother had prescience magic also, but she said mine is the most powerful the family has ever seen."

The beastkin must be pulling their hair out looking for Amako right now.

I had the strong sense that things were about to get very complicated. Probably the whole reason Rose had shut her down was that her vision had something to do with her standing in the Beastlands.

And if she brought Rose her story while the captain was preparing for the Demon Lord's attempted invasion, of course the woman was going to shut her down.

"In any case, it's Usato-kun's call now."

And he wasn't the type to shut anyone down.

* * *

"Let me get this straight," said Rose with an annoyed sigh. "A fox beastkin says her mommy is sick, and she wants you to go heal her?"

"In short, yes."

Rose sat in a wooden chair in her neatly organized office.

"You've brought me one heck of a problem, that's for sure. The beastkin all look the same to me, but you bring me a time-reading princess? Get the heck out of here."

"Time-reading . . . princess?"

That really *did* sound like one heck of a problem.

"Some beastkin have a rare magic known widely as time-reading magic. Beastkin with this magic play an important role—they see disasters coming, and they warn everyone of them. If a girl like that is here, in the Llinger Kingdom, it may cause the Beastlands to take a hostile stance against us. I mean, they already don't think much of us as it is."

"Even now, while the Demon Lord's army might invade at any moment?" I asked.

"Well, the beastkin hate us more than they hate the demons."

I'd had a feeling that Amako was something special to her people, but I hadn't imagined this. I was glad I brought the topic to Rose first. Who knows what trouble I'd have gotten in if I'd just gone galivanting outside of the kingdom?

"What's your opinion on it all, Captain?" I asked.

"I want to flat out say no, but I can't make that decision without conferring with King Lloyd. The thing is . . . we won't be able to see him for a few days because he's arranging for a way to bring in the support of other countries.

A few days? What am I supposed to do until then?

Should I ask Amako for more details, or should I start training to prepare?

"In the meantime, you'll be training," said Rose, answering my internal monologue for me. "Even if King Lloyd *does* let you go to the Beastlands, as it stands, you'll have a hard enough time just looking after yourself. So I'll toughen you up. I don't expect us to see many folks in need of healing anyway."

"I mean, I don't really mind, but . . ."

The fact that I didn't react with revulsion made me wonder if maybe I was pretty used to this treatment.

Wait a sec. Was I getting used to it? Wouldn't being used to this kind of abuse make me a grade-A masochist?

I felt some self-disgust rising up in me at just how accustomed I was to Rose's "training," but then I remembered I was in her office and kept myself in check. I didn't want her getting mad at me here.

"In that case," I said, going on, "I'll let senpai and Amako know. They're still waiting downstairs."

Rose grunted. I gave a brisk salute, then headed downstairs.

Once back at the food hall, I spotted Inukami-senpai doing her utmost to engage Amako in conversation.

I glanced at Amako. She had a head of golden hair with a natural luster to it that was clearly different from dyed hair, and she was about a head shorter than senpai.

It really is a wonder that she made it all this way on her own.

I walked over to them so I could get them up to speed with what Rose had told me, but Amako turned to me and replied before I'd even spoken a word.

"Yep. It's going to take a little time," she said, watching me carefully.

She'd already seen with her prescience what I was going to tell them. Inukami-senpai, however, had not.

"So you two are just communicating through eyesight alone now?" she said, confused. "Damn, that stings. Makes me feel like I'm on the back foot."

"Why are you even making this a competition? All I came to say was that it'll take some time before we can get an audience with the king. You make it sound like I'm some kind of criminal."

Is she **trying** *to make me into some kind of criminal? Wait, are Lolita complexes even a thing in this world?*

Inukami-senpai looked away, a slight sadness on her face.

"You barely even notice me these days. I feel so neglected I could cry."

"You're fine if you can say as much. If you're feeling neglected, that just means that we've gotten close enough for you to feel that way, no?"

"You know, you and I, we have different concepts of the word 'close.'"

"What are you talking about? I look after you just fine, don't I?"

"Why are you making me sound like some kind of pet dog?!"

Uh . . . because that's exactly how you act? And then there's that dogged curiosity . . .

Senpai had a lot she wanted to get off her chest, but I sat her back down and turned to Amako.

"So what now?" I asked.

"I didn't think we'd be able to leave right away," replied Amako. "So I'll head home."

"Speaking of which, where do you live?" I asked.

"The old lady who runs the fruit shop is letting me live with her."

"Oh, *that's* where you're staying?"

I remembered seeing a place selling spiky fruit right before Rose launched me into the forest. That was the place Amako was calling home for the time being. And if she'd been staying there until now, it must have been pretty comfortable. That at least was something of a relief.

And as for me? Should I go see Orga or get straight to training?

I could see senpai staring at me with that expectation in her eyes, so I decided I'd head to the infirmary like I'd originally planned.

"I was thinking of heading to town anyway, so I'll go with you," I said.

"Okay."

"You're coming too, right, Inukami-senpai?"

"I am! I am!" she yipped.

And she complains about being called a pet dog . . .

I took off my Rescue Team coat and hung it on a chair. I'd leave Blurin here this time.

"Usato?" said Amako.

"Hm?"

Amako was standing in front of me, staring intently into my eyes. They were such a beautiful blue. I was just thinking about how nice people's eyes were in this world when—

"Thank you," she said.

The hint of a smile rose to her face.

"That's my line," I said, smiling back.

Because of you, senpai and Kazuki are both still here.

A strange expression grew upon Inukami-senpai's face, and though Amako remained expressionless, there was a lightness to her step now.

The three of us headed for town.

Just as we were about to reach the entrance to town, Amako remembered something and turned around to look at Inukami-senpai and me. We looked at her, puzzled.

"I forgot to mention," she said as if warning us, "that the two of you get totally mobbed by everyone."

And then she took off running. I stood there, mouth agape, just watching her.

"Huh? What does she mean 'everyone'?"

Amako disappeared into the distance as Inukami-senpai gave me a hesitant tap on the shoulder. I looked around to see that the townsfolk were closing in, all of them filled with joy and clutching bags filled with produce they intended to thrust upon us.

"Usato-kun . . ." muttered senpai. "How do you think we look to everyone right now? Do you think we look like a couple?"

"Master and servant, more likely. But shouldn't you, uh . . . shouldn't you be a little more worried?"

I hadn't run around town all those times doing absolutely nothing. I knew many of its citizens now and often talked with them. I was painfully aware of how tight-knit they were.

"Amako . . ." I muttered as I heaved a sigh, "couldn't you have told us about this earlier?"

I prepared myself for the incoming uproar.

CHAPTER 4

A Return to Hell!

I stood with Rose on the Rescue Team training grounds. I was wearing my branded training gear and was stretching so I'd be ready to go at a moment's notice. Rose, however, stood silently in front of me with her arms crossed. She was thinking about something very carefully as she looked at me.

"I was thinking I'd just put you through some training exercises today, but as far as your healing magic goes, frankly, I don't have much for you," she said.

"Huh? But I still can't heal illnesses or more complicated injuries," I replied.

"You'll work that out on your own as you get more used to your magic. As it stands, you're still not ready for that."

Man, talk about shooting a guy's confidence down in one fell swoop.

If that were true, what else was I supposed to do? Was she just going to tell me to work out again? I felt like I'd maxed that out, which meant it was about time to think of something new.

"To be frank . . . well, you're just on the cusp of having the right strength and stamina levels, which is enough for the time being," she told me.

In other words: I still wasn't nearly strong enough.

Just how far does this woman want to push me?

"So then, what are we doing?" I asked.

Rose took a step back and began swinging her arms as a kind of warm-up.

I immediately got a really bad feeling about it. It was like a vague chill running down my spine. Rose, meanwhile, cracked her knuckles with a grin on her face.

"I'm going to hit you," she said.

I laughed.

"Yeah, but seriously though . . ."

"I'm going to hit you, right now. It will be faster than you can react. But try to get out of the way."

"Do you hate me? Is that what this is?! If I eat one of your punches, I'll turn to dust!"

In the back of my mind, I saw Rose caving in that giant snake's skull. I couldn't even make a scratch on its scales, and she **crushed** it like it was nothing.

You hit a person with a punch like that and it's game over.

"You rely on your healing magic too much," Rose said. "And yeah, I was the one who trained you that way, but we are ready for the next step."

Punching me is the next step?! That doesn't even make sense?!

I tried to make a getaway, but she had me by the collar before I got anywhere.

"Yeah, no!" I cried. "You'll kill me! Amako! Didn't you see *this* future?!"

"Until now, your defense has been practically nonexistent. You've managed to make things work, I'll give you that, but healing magic won't work on injuries that have been cursed . . . so you gotta learn to dodge and weave."

I have zero confidence in my ability to do that. And didn't you say you'd hit me faster than I **can** *do that, anyway?!*

And I knew that when it came to this woman, she'd use healing magic as an excuse to not pull any of her punches.

"But hey," said Rose, "I'm no monster. I'll go easy to start with."

"Uh, no. Things went off the rails the moment you talked about hitting your staff. Are you completely out of your mind, you . . . Uh, I mean, I'm sorry."

"Oh, I get it now," said Rose. "You want a taste of full strength. And I am all too happy to oblige! I **love** that you love your training!"

Why does my mouth always work against me like that?

Rose gripped my hand, then threw me up in the air. I let out a nervous chuckle in response and covered myself in my healing magic. As I felt myself fly through the air, I saw that I was going to land about ten meters from where I was standing. At the last second, I managed to land on my feet. At the same time, I brought my arms up to protect my head and my heart.

"I said no defense," said Rose.

"Wait, are you . . ."

And then a shock ran through my body unlike anything I had ever felt. I thought she'd put a hole in me it was so painful. Up and down suddenly reversed. The world spun, and I felt like I was going to be sick as I flew through the air again.

"Are you out of your . . . ?!"

Later, I would be able to say this much:

I had never taken a hit like that in my whole life.

I came to under the tree next to the training grounds. I was blanketed in the pleasant shade of its leaves. It was nice. I imagined Rose had never given me a beatdown and claimed it was "training."

Have I been working too hard? Is that where the nightmare came from? Rose is nicer now, and here I am, still with this horrible impression of her. Can't have that. It's like Ururu said. She's fragile. I can't live my whole life being scared of her. Nope.

"Awake, are you? Alright, get up and let's go again," Rose said.

And just like that, I had to give up my dreams and face reality again. Everything I'd thought since coming to and the stuff that Ururu said? Delusional lies.

Time to face reality and get back into training. Surely, that's the easiest way to get back into it.

"Okay . . ." I said.

Yep. Just because I wasn't injured didn't mean I could say it was all a dream. It was just like Rose to take such good care of me. She was the true portrait of a teacher. She was far too good a teacher for the likes of me.

So good I wish she'd take on a different pupil.

"Relax, Usato. I went easy on you," said Rose. "No injuries, right?"

"Um, thanks?"

But the whole while, I was thinking one thing: *You really are a monster.*

That day, Rose ended up just punching me over and over again. A few times I thought I could almost dodge out of the way, but then Rose would speed up and I'd get smacked all over the training grounds. If this was what she called going easy, then I was terrified.

That said, I *did* feel like my stamina improved.

And I felt it even more after the following days. I really felt like I could withstand some hefty attacks. In old-world terms, it was like being able to stand up against a missile without breaking a sweat.

I mean, I was only 170 centimeters tall, you know. And I was about regular weight for my height. Just a regular guy getting thrown from one end of the training grounds to the other, eating punches that sent me flying through the air. I'd gotten to the point that most attacks just didn't faze me anymore.

In the last half of the training, right when I'd think about dodging, she'd slam me with a critical hit.

I legitimately think Rose might have forgotten the point of the training.

* * *

Just like that, I'd been through four days of Rose's training. She gave me a break, and so I headed for the castle. Rose had some errands to run, which meant I had a day to myself.

I didn't have any particular business at the castle; I just wanted to drop in on someone I was curious about. I ended up talking all about my recent training.

"So then, get this," I said. "The captain sent me soaring through the air with a punch—over and over again. She's awful."

"What are you doing here, seriously?" asked the black knight.

That's where I was: standing at the black knight's cell, unloading my woes.

"Oh, I just wondered how you were doing," I said.

The knight didn't show her face. She was just sitting in a corner of her cell in full armor. She'd been peaceful and quiet ever since I'd healed her. Still, the kingdom was at a loss for what to do with her. Some people were of the mindset that if she was dangerous, then we should execute her. But the king flatly refused that idea. You could say he was being soft, but I agreed with him, personally. I didn't want the kingdom to be a place with the death penalty.

"What are you going to do?" I asked.

"I dunno . . . Just stay here, I guess," she replied.

"Are you okay with that?"

"Does it matter? I don't get to decide."

It was a good point. But I still wondered what was going to happen to her. After all, I was the one who captured her, so I felt invested. If she *did* get executed, I'd feel awful.

"You, uh . . ." she started.

"Hm?"

"No, it's nothing. Are we done here?"

"Alright, I get it," I said, standing up and leaving the cell.

I wonder if I can ask Rose about the black knight. But also, it seems like she's got some plans of her own with the black knight. Maybe there's no need for me to do anything.

I walked through the castle with my head full of thoughts about the black knight. That was when I noticed a figure practicing sword work outside. I knew it was probably Kazuki, so I walked over to say hello.

I could hear him grunt with each swing of his sword. He was working really hard. I didn't want to disturb him while he was so focused, so I moved to the shade of a tree. I saw Celia there, grinning as she watched Kazuki training.

"Oh," she said, noticing me. "Hello, Usato-sama."

"Hi, Celia-sama," I replied. "How long has he been at it?"

"Since well before I got here. I'm starting to worry that he'll wear himself out. I think the battle with the Demon Lord's forces has lit a fire in him. He's been training much harder since he returned to the castle."

"That's weird," I said. "Shouldn't training be a more grueling, torturous, and painful ordeal?"

"Are you okay? Usato-sama, what is that look in your eyes?" asked Celia-sama. She was smiling but she'd suddenly gone pale. "It's quite . . . frightening."

My eyes? I wonder how I must have looked. I guess the word "training" triggered something in me that brought to mind what Rose always put me through. In any case, I turned my attention back on Kazuki. His form was excellent. He looked really cool.

"Oh? Is that you, Usato?" he said, noticing me.

Kazuki put his sword back in its sheath and took a nearby cloth to wipe the sweat from his brow, then ran over to us.

"Long time no see!" he said.

"Sorry, I've been caught up with my own training too," I replied.

Well, if you can call what Rose does to me training, anyway.

"Inukami-senpai told me that you're hoping to help a beastkin by going with her to the Beastlands."

"Well, first up, the king must have a say in it all before I do anything. But I do want to help her if I can."

"Er . . . about that . . ." said Celia-sama.

She looked like she had something on her mind. She was the daughter of the king, so there was probably a lot more she was in the know about.

"About your wish to go to the Beastlands," she said. "I believe you will be granted permission."

It hadn't even been a week yet. Had things already been decided? I had a feeling it was all moving too fast. Something was up.

"My father is sending letters to various other nations for support in the fight against the Demon Lord's army. It's likely you will be asked to deliver a letter from him to the beastkin people."

But why me? Why ask me to deliver a letter from the king? Wouldn't he choose senpai or Kazuki first?

Well, whatever. I'm sure he'll explain it to me himself later. Best focus on Celia-sama for now.

"When we fought the Demon Lord's army before—before you, Suzune-sama, and Kazuki-sama came—we were unable to gain the help of the beastkin people. But the situation was a little different from the battle we just had."

"Different? How so?" I asked.

"We succeeded in fighting off the Demon Lord's army, but even with Suzune-sama and Kazuki-sama's strength on our side, it was still a hard-fought battle. Without them, the casualty count would have been even higher."

"Well, yeah," said Kazuki, "and if Usato hadn't saved my life in that last battle, I would have . . . uh, oops."

Kazuki covered his mouth with a hand. I couldn't work it out. He was keeping a close eye on Celia-sama's reaction.

Wait, don't tell me he didn't tell her that he almost died.

But more importantly, I was concerned with the letter the king intended to send. Was it okay to tell them that without Amako's vision, we would have lost that last battle? If we did mention it, perhaps it would help convince other nations that the Demon Lord's army was truly dangerous and push them into lending a hand.

"Nothing has been officially confirmed just yet," said Celia-sama, "but the king will definitely send letters to each nation. I know it may be something of a burden for you, Usato-sama, but . . ."

"I already owe the kingdom for looking after me," I said. "A little burden like that is nothing in comparison."

And it would be like heaven compared to the training Rose had planned for me.

Wait, why am I making decisions based on the severity of Rose's training?

Well, in any case, it's not like I'm wrong.

"I guess I'll just wait to hear the details from the king later," I said. "In the meantime, I'll stay ready and keep on training. Which reminds me, I should probably get going."

"What? Leaving already?" cried Kazuki.

Celia-sama giggled.

"Kazuki-sama," she said, "you know that Usato-sama probably has places to go and things to do."

Well, I didn't have either that day, but seeing Kazuki training had gotten me pumped to go and do something myself. I couldn't have imagined that wanting to visit the Beastlands to help Amako's mother might turn into a quest to deliver letters across the world. Still, I knew it was a task of huge importance.

The Llinger Kingdom was, for all intents and purposes, the front lines. It was the closest place to the territory controlled by the Demon Lord. This was why we needed the help of our neighbors, but . . . it was probably also why many of them had forgotten the danger of the Demon Lord's invasion.

But if there were no Inukami-senpai, no Kazuki, and no Amako, the kingdom would have crumbled, and they would have received the message loud and clear. The thought sent a chill down my spine.

"As for us, Kazuki-sama," said Celia-sama, "would you mind telling me in more detail what it was you said earlier about being saved?"

"Um, er . . . pardon?"

"In great detail, please."

Kazuki laughed nervously.

"Er . . . sorry."

I chuckled as I listened to their conversation begin, but I was already heading back to the Rescue Team training grounds.

* * *

Today that healer, Usato, came by. He unloaded his complaints on me, and then he left. What was he even trying to do? Was he checking up on me to make sure I didn't run away? Even if I tried that, the Llinger forces would be after me like a flash, but even if I made it back to the Demon Lord's army, there was only my boring old life to look forward to.

Not that I was particularly keen on being executed. If they put me in magic lockdown restraints, then I'd have no way to use my armor—I'd be powerless. But just being scrubbed out of existence kind of rubbed me the wrong way too.

Maybe if it looked like I was going to be killed, I'd just cause a ruckus until the healer came.

"Well, it's an idea, at least," I said out loud.

But I could wrap my head around the people here. They didn't torture me, and their security was really lax. Were they really trying to keep me locked up? But then the actual cell and surrounding architecture were really solid. It all agitated me to no end. It was like, do you want to keep me in or do you want me to escape? I wished they'd be more consistent.

But the weirdest one had to be Usato. He healed my wounds and he made a point of coming to see me—I couldn't make heads or tails of the guy.

"What am I going to do?" I muttered.

I let my armor fade so I could feel the air on my body. The cell wasn't particularly hot or cold, but it felt nice. I leaned back against the wall.

Go back to the Demon Lord and return to long days of boredom, or stay here, locked up in this cell. I didn't actually mind staying in the cell, but it bothered me that Usato came to see me. Nobody had ever actually tried getting to know me before. I didn't know what I was supposed to do.

"Why am I even thinking about getting to know that guy?" I grumbled.

He was my enemy. Nothing had changed that.

And yet . . .

Suddenly, I became aware of footsteps coming down the stairs that led to my cell. At first, I thought it was a knight on guard duty. But then I remembered that they wore armor, and there was a unique metallic sound that came with their footfalls. I hid my face under my helmet and glared at the staircase.

From the darkness came a woman in a white coat with green hair and a scar over her right eye. She matched the description Usato had given me of his captain. This was the human that the third army commander was so worried about—the other healer.

"Yo," she said.

It was the Rescue Team captain, Rose.

"King Lloyd asked me to come. Not much of a talker, are you?"

"What do you want?" I asked.

Rose pulled a nearby chair over near the cell and slumped into it. She looked at me as the corners of her lips curled up. I could tell by the fear her eyes struck in me that she really was Usato's superior, but I stared right back at her anyway.

"You got two choices," said Rose, sticking up her index and middle finger.

"Two?"

"One: You spend your life right here."

Life in this cell. It would, admittedly, be difficult for me to break out of this cell with my magic. On the other hand, if I was going to be executed, I'd fight back with everything I had.

"Now, I don't mind if that's your choice, but King Lloyd did have another suggestion."

"Hm?"

Rose held only a single finger up now.

Go on, say it. You want to kill me.

"If you're going to kill me, hurry up and do it already."

"Hey now, let's not get ahead of ourselves. Impatient one, aren't ya?"

Rose stood up, took a key from her pocket, then unlocked the cell door and came inside.

"King Lloyd's other option—and it's a pain in the ass, but still—is for me to help you turn over a new leaf. Basically, make you into an upstanding demon citizen."

"What? Are all of you crazy or is it just that you're stu—urk!"

I felt a sudden shock against my skull and my helmet vanished completely. I looked up as tears reflexively welled in my eyes and saw Rose looking down on me. She'd just hit me with the edge of her hand, like a blade. She looked somewhat impressed.

"So healing magic really *is* effective," she said. "Not that we need it now."

There wasn't any pain, but my head throbbed as my body was lifted back up.

"King Lloyd isn't a big fan of executing his prisoners. Even if it's a dangerous hag like y'self."

And that was what made this method all the crazier. Even though it was a chance for me, it was still way too lenient. And I would have said as much if the woman standing before me didn't freeze my vocal cords with sheer fear.

Rose continued. "Now, I am well aware of how loyal demons are to their brethren. And we may well be enemies, but if we execute a prisoner in cold blood, we'd just incite rage in the Demon Lord's army. Nothing more painful and troublesome to deal with than demons drunk on vengeance. Right?"

Rose lifted me up as she asked me the question. I couldn't stop sweating. She must have been way more powerful than Usato, because the moment she touched me, my armor dissipated. Without anything else to grab, she grabbed me by my shirt and attached a collar to my neck. The magic that flowed from the center of my body seemed to stop in an instant, and the rest of my armor vanished.

"Huh?" I said.

"Truth is, the kingdom doesn't have the resources to have someone watch over you day and night, so life imprisonment for you is out of the question. That means option number two."

"What? No . . . wait . . ."

"Your magic is sealed by that magical accessory on your neck. Impressive, no?"

You're not supposed to be able to use something so powerful so casually?!

Magic accessories were incredibly rare and she'd used one on me like it was nothing. Panic rushed through me and I froze in fear.

"Originally, we were gonna put this accessory on you and just leave you here. But that'd just be putting off the problem. So King Lloyd gave me my orders. He said he'd leave the black knight's fate in my hands."

Rose's face in that moment was more terrifying than any monster I had ever seen.

"Huh, wait, what . . . No! Let me go! You brute! Put me back in my cell!"

"You don't get a choice."

Rose then flicked me in the forehead, right between the eyes, so hard my vision wavered.

"Whaha?!" I exclaimed, my sight blurring with tears.

"As of today, we're breaking you in, so get ready. You're joining the Rescue Team, and you're starting from rock bottom," said Rose, cackling. "You know? Building up a demon? That sounds very intriguing."

Everything was happening too fast. I couldn't follow. This nation wasn't lenient. Not in the slightest. And as Rose carried me easily on her shoulder and up the stairs, I felt, for the first time in my life, true terror.

* * *

"Blurin! We're doing another lap!" I shouted.

Blurin growled. We'd been running and running and had just gotten back to the training grounds. Usually, I used my healing magic for this kind of thing, but I'd opted to go without it this time. I wasn't doing it for any reason in particular. I guess I'd just been thinking recently that the key to training was trying lots of new things.

I already knew that running without the healing magic made my body tired. And I had a feeling I now understood what Rose meant when she said, "You're on the cusp of having the right strength and stamina levels," and that I relied too much on my healing magic.

I knew now that I had to be able to move well even without my magic. If some enemy turned up who could seal my magic, the only thing I'd have to fall back on was my only physical abilities.

"Now I get it," I said. "*That's* why she beat the heck out of me. The captain wanted me to understand this for myself!"

Of course, my healing magic was important. But at the heart of the Rescue Team was physical training. I could see now that all the training I'd done up until this point really was the best training I could have asked for, and—

"Ya got it all wrong, idiot!" shouted Rose, coming out of nowhere.

For good measure, she also kicked me. I flipped a full three times. When I finally got back to my feet, Rose sighed.

"I thought I told you to take today off!"

"Well, yeah, but I couldn't just sit around doing nothing, and . . . Huh?"

It was then that I noticed Rose carrying someone on her shoulder. The body didn't move, but at least it was breathing, which at least meant it was alive. It didn't look like we'd be having that for dinner tonight . . . which, of course, was a terrifying idea.

But wait, I've seen that silver hair before. She looks just like the black knight who was locked up in that basement cell.

"Huh?! Seriously?!" I exclaimed.

"Shut up," Rose said, smacking me as she dropped the silver-haired girl on the ground.

"How?!"

The girl was pale and looked confused as she lifted her head and looked straight at me. She was so shocked she was speechless.

I was no different.

The girl had horns growing from her head, silver hair, and tanned skin. She was supposed to be in the basement dungeons, out of harm's way—so what was she doing right here in front of me?! I looked to Rose for an explanation.

"Do you have any idea who this is?!" I cried. "This is the girl inside the black knight armor!"

"Yep, she's a demon. Intriguing, huh? She looks tough too. Worth training, in other words."

"Wait wait wait!"

Intriguing?! Did she just bring this person here on a whim?!

"Her magic is sealed so it's not like she can do anything," said Rose. "And besides, I'll be keeping an eye on her myself."

"Well, at least that's a relief," I said.

I wish she'd said that earlier though. Then I wouldn't have gotten so worked up about it all. I let out a sigh of relief and looked over at the girl, who was watching our back-and-forth with a dumbfounded look on her face.

"What even is this?" she asked. "What's going to happen to me?"

"Well, for starters, how about writing a diary?" I said.

I had a feeling that in a couple of days, she'd be looking for ways to escape reality.

* * *

Day One

Usato gave me a diary. I don't know why, but I figure I'll write down what happens starting today. It's been a while since I wrote anything, but I remember how to do it better than I expected.

That woman ripped me from my cell and took me to some place she called the Rescue Team headquarters. I have a collar on that seals my magic powers, and I can't get it off no matter what I do. Ever since it was closed, the clasp keeps warping and changing shape.

That's pretty much all that happened today.

Rose is going to start my training tomorrow. But whatever. I'm a demon. Human training is going to be a cakewalk for me. I'm not worried about a thing.

Day Two

I thought I was going to die.

I made a horrible mistake. I thought we were doing human training, but I got it all wrong. I was made to run an excessive distance with these two ogres called Tong and Alec and these two goblins called Gomul and Gurd. It was beyond excruciating.

I told them they were all monsters, but they insisted that they're human. But if you ask me, they're monsters that Rose *is raising like pets. I almost feel sorry for them—they really think they're human.*

I'm better physically equipped than most humans, but among demons, I'm not particularly strong. When the sun was at its height, I collapsed from exhaustion. I don't know if Rose *was waiting for me to do that, but she came out of nowhere and gave my legs a slap and forced me back on my feet. All the pain went away, but it still hurt, just not on a physical level.*

I heard her mumbling. I only caught the words "worse than" and "Usa," but my eyes were all watery for some reason and I couldn't focus on what she was saying.

This place is hell. I want to go back to my cell.

Day Three

I can't move my body.

Day Four

That woman is inhuman. She's crazy. She kicked me and made me run even though my body won't listen to me.

And why was Usato laughing?

They said this is par for the course. Insanity.

You're all bonkers.

Day Five

Today Usato came running with us. It was weird. He was running with ogres and goblins, but he never looked tired. It's so hard for me. Usato must be inhuman too. But that makes sense; no human could take down the likes of me.

That's what I told myself. But then I remembered that only humans can be healers.

So Usato is a human, but he's also inhuman.

That's my understanding of it.

Day Six

When training started, I heard a crashing sound come from the forest. Each time it happened, birds would go flying from the same area. I could see a big tree shaking in the distance.

Tomorrow I'm going to fake that I'm tired so I can go check it out.

Nobody is better at slacking off than me.

Day Seven

Day Eight

I am sorry for trying to be a slacker.

Day Nine

This might sound unbelievable, but Rose is punching Usato with incredible force. She calls it training. Every time he gets hit, Usato spins and goes flying and then he collides with the trees, after which he bounces on the ground a few times before finally coming to a stop.

I thought he was dead. For real.

Even ogres—which are mega powerful—don't make that kind of a sound when they hit people. He took a **direct** *hit right to the center of his body. But Usato just got up and held his healing magic over his stomach and looked kind of hurt. That's it.*

I couldn't believe it, even though I saw it with my own eyes. If I don't write it down here, I don't think I'll believe even myself. Are we in Demon Lord territory? This surpasses even what happens **there**.

I think I'm going crazy.

Day Ten

For whatever reason, Rose thinks I'm interested in Usato's training. Tonight during dinner she said I could go along with his training tomorrow. Honestly, I was so tired from training with the ogres and goblins that I don't think I said anything clear in my reply.

Still, this might be my chance. I was brought here against my will, but Usato's training has always been unknown to me. Now I'll get to see it. Yesterday I had to have been daydreaming—no human can do that. But this time, I'll work out the secret to his strength.

Usato didn't like Rose's suggestion at all . . . Looks like he doesn't want me to know. It felt good seeing him look like that.

I'm freaking exhausted, but at least I'll sleep well tonight.

I shut my diary. I'd accidentally brought it to the training grounds. Then I opened it again to double-check what I'd written and closed it again.

I must have been dreaming again.

I wanted desperately for someone to wake me from the torture playing out before my eyes. Torture they called "training."

"I told you to dodge! The only thing you seem to be able to do well is eat my shots!" Rose shouted.

"You keep shifting your angle of attack every time I try! How in the world do you expect me to dodge that?!" Usato exclaimed.

"You telling me you can't look with your eyes and just dodge, you idiot?!"

"How could anyone **just** dodge?!"

Usato had been hit so hard he flew off into the distance, but he jumped back to his feet like it was nothing and verbally blasted her. Over the last few days, a fear of that woman was carved into my very being, and seeing Usato not even flinch when she grabbed his head in her hands made me tremble.

"Tch," spat Rose. "One more time, then."

"You think *you're* frustrated? You don't know the half of it," he spat back.

Rose and Usato both returned to their spots on the training ground, glaring at each other. There were ten meters between them. Usato stood on one side, his feet slightly apart and his eyes burning a hole into Rose. She stared right back at him, her eyes narrowed.

Hers weren't the eyes of a human. The third army's commander was stronger than I thought. Not just anyone could face off against a monster like this. Sure, there were magic types to consider, but I knew that I didn't stand a chance.

The moment my thoughts trailed off, Rose vanished. I couldn't see her at all. It was different from before when I'd been able to see her. I turned to Usato.

"Whoa!" he shouted.

In an instant, Rose had appeared in front of him, her fist flying through the air. But Usato had twisted and evaded the blow.

"Huh? You dodged it?" I uttered.

I couldn't believe it.

Did he see her punch . . . and then dodge it?

Whatever the case, that was beyond human.

"I . . . I did it! This means . . ."

"Don't let your guard down," said Rose.

Usato had felt unbridled joy at evading Rose's attack only to eat a follow-up spin kick right to the guts. He let out a groan of surprise as he was hit with a force that sounded like way too much power for any single body to take. He spun through the air, cutting a neat arc, then bounced off the ground four times.

It was the work of a monster.

"Are you . . . Are you okay?" I muttered, worried, even though it was entirely out of character for me.

But Usato jumped to his feet, clutching his stomach. He was a little wobbly on his feet, so it looked like he'd taken damage. I rushed over to him to see if he was okay. He lifted up his head and raised both his fists high into the air like he didn't even know I was right there.

"Woohooo!" he shouted. "I did it!"

"Wha . . ."

I was shocked at the sudden victory cry, but even more shocked that he was so unfazed by Rose's kick.

"You did good," said Rose, letting out a sigh of relief. "Now I don't have to hit you anymore. You're free to return to your usual training."

Usato bowed as Rose stood before him, her arms crossed and a smile on her face.

"Thank you, Captain!"

Perhaps it was because I'd seen how fiercely they were facing off just moments ago, but I broke out in a cold sweat. Rose said she had work to do back at the main building and that I should do whatever training Usato said I should do.

"She's a real monster, changing the trajectory of her punches like that," he said.

"I wonder if you realize you're turning into a monster too?"

"Hm? Did you say something?"

I let out a deep sigh as Usato moved to a corner of the training grounds. He sat down among a bunch of baggage, then picked up a coat of some kind and put it on.

"Well, seeing as you're tagging along today, let's go for a light jog," he said. "Oh, speaking of which, I know it's kind of late, but can I ask you something?"

"What?"

"What's your name?"

"You waited until now?"

"Well, I meant to ask earlier, but after food and chores and stuff, you're usually straight to bed."

He was right. These past ten days, he'd never needed to even know my name. It kind of vexed me.

"My name, huh . . ."

Except for the second army's commander, pretty much everyone just called me the black knight. I knew I'd told Rose what my name was, but when I thought about it, I realized that she'd never called me by name in front of Usato.

It's been a while since anyone has asked me my name.

"Felm . . ." I said, a little nervously. "My parents called me Fel."

"Felm," said Usato, nodding. "Got it. Well, get ready because we're going running."

"Oi."

"Hm?"

"Is that it?"

"Yeah, I think that's it?"

I didn't like his attitude. Like he didn't really care. I kicked him in the shin and started warming up. It was a pretty good kick, but he didn't look fazed in the slightest. In fact, he started jumping on the spot.

Damn you.

"A light jog is fine, right?" he asked.

"Don't belittle me," I spat. "I'm fast enough to keep up with those other beasts now."

"Yeah, but just keeping up with them is not really good enough, you know?"

He said it all with a smile on his face and then he took off at an easy pace.

"What?"

You dare to look down on me? I am not the sort of demon to just take that kind of treatment sitting down, you know.

I felt the corners of my mouth turn up as I took off after him.

"Right from the beginning, I never liked you much," I said as I picked up speed and passed Usato. But Usato just laughed and caught up with me, still wearing that annoying grin.

"We don't know each other well enough for you to like me, no?" he said.

One thing I'd learned in my ten days of being here was that this guy, too, was a monster.

"Damn you!" I shouted, picking up the pace again.

"Hey, wait," said Usato. "I thought I was setting the pace?"

"Shut up! I will never . . . NEVER . . . lose to you!"

Even if it's by guts and willpower alone, I will beat you. You cocky healer. I will show you the difference between demons and humans!

* * *

"Hey, Usato."

"Yes?"

"I left you with the weakling," said Rose. "What happened?"

Training was done for the day and we were all at the table, eating dinner. Well, everyone was there but Felm, whose chair was empty.

"Uh, she fainted," I said with a wry grin.

"She fainted?"

After I'd finished training with Rose, we'd gone running. But Felm was so hyper-competitive that she'd run at a full sprint and, as a result, fainted.

"She's okay," I said. "I healed her and took her to her room."

"Well, I don't want to deal with her fainting on me tomorrow," said Rose, frustration in her voice as she pushed a palm into her forehead. "So make sure you take her food to her after dinner."

"Yes, Captain."

"Please tell me she's not being a tsundere. . ." muttered Rose.

I looked at the empty chair beside me. Felm was more of a kid than I'd first thought. It was clear enough in how competitive she was with me, but also in her disregard for her own physical condition.

"Oh man! Did the princess faint?!" said Gomul, cackling with laughter. "You don't know how to go easy, do you, Usato?"

"We just went running!" I said. "Just ordinary, everyday running!"

"What you call ordinary everyone else calls insane! It's inhuman to be like you."

"Shut up! I'm more human than the captain is!" I retorted.

Like I'm just going to sit here and let you call me a monster!

I stood up from my chair, glaring at Gomul.

Then something whizzed through the air past my face. I looked behind me and saw a spoon stabbed deep into the wooden wall. When I turned around, I found Rose watching me with an ice-cold grin on her face. I healed the cut on the side of my face, then made eye contact with Gomul.

"Gomul-kun," I said, "talking that way to people is not very nice. However, I too could have been nicer with my choice of words. I apologize."

"I said too much when I said you were inhuman," said Gomul. "I also totally apologize."

Everyone in the Rescue Team is friends, we thought as we glanced timidly at Rose, who appeared to have forgiven us.

Phew, at least we managed to escape that without punishment.

But hang on . . . are spoons sharp enough to stab into walls?

"We've trained with her for ten days now, but she ain't as strong as most demons," said Alec. He ate his food with manners completely out of place with his frightening demeanor. "How you planning to toughen her up, Sister Rose?"

"Yeah, that girl was born with a silver spoon in her mouth when it comes to magic, but if we break her, she'll come round.

Right, Tong?"

"Let it go, would you?" he said.

Tong looked away, suddenly awkward. He was an old hand with the Rescue Team and had probably been through a lot.

"Tong, did you do something to the captain?" I asked.

"Shut yer trap. It's none of yer business!" said Tong, shutting down my prying question.

It must have been some embarrassing moment in the past he didn't want to see the light of day. I figured I'd just ask Alec or someone else about it later. That's what I decided as I washed my last piece of bread down with the rest of my soup.

"Usato," said Rose.

"Yes?"

What is it this time? New training? Surely there's nothing more grueling than what I just went through . . . right?

"Go to the castle first thing tomorrow morning. King Lloyd wants to talk to you and the heroes."

"You mean . . . ?"

"Yep. He's decided what the Llinger Kingdom is going to do next."

Which means the letters to the other nations would be going out pretty soon. I was just glad that I'd completed Rose's training with a little time to spare. My endurance and reaction speeds had improved, and I'd be able to survive most battles, so long as I wasn't up against any crazy monsters.

Wait a second. That training was supposed to hone my evasive abilities. But my endurance went up. Probably not worth lingering on.

"I'm guessing I should take Amako with me too."

"That's part of it. Don't forget to take her."

Huh? Does the king want to meet her?

In any case, I'd just go pick her up before going to the castle. I cleaned up my plate and thought about the immediate future. Yeah, there was the actual passing out of the letters to think about, but there was lots we'd have to be careful of on the way—things like areas we needed to avoid, villages and other colonies, and even treacherous mountains.

"I'm going to have to study the geography of this place," I muttered.

Perhaps I could ask Welcie to show me a map of the way to the Beastlands.

"Alright, then I guess I'm headed to the castle tomorrow. Thanks for dinner," I said.

I tidied up my cutlery and left the food hall.

An early morning meant an early night, but before that, I had to make sure Felm ate her dinner. She was probably still sleeping.

"Guess I'll just wake her up," I said to myself.

It wasn't like Felm was injured. My healing magic fixed any wound or exhaustion that wasn't either a curse or mental fatigue. That meant that, right now, she was just sleeping the time away.

I wasn't the type of monster (like Rose) to force an unconscious person awake and make them go running. I'd put Felm to bed, but when I thought about tomorrow, I knew it was best to wake her up. I knocked on her door. Her room was the Rescue Team storeroom, but it had been used by Orga and Ururu in the past. The day after Felm arrived, we'd cleaned it up to make it livable, but hopefully she hadn't messed it up.

There was no response to my knocks.

"I guess she's still sleeping," I muttered with a sigh.

I opened the door to find Felm at her desk in the corner, writing by the light of a single candle that illuminated the otherwise desolate room. She was scribbling something quite hurriedly, and I wondered why she hadn't come down to dinner if she was awake. She didn't even realize I was there. Instead, she groaned occasionally and shook her head as she wrote.

"Oi, Felm," I said.

She fell from her chair with a crash and a scream. I couldn't help but chuckle. I picked up the notebook that had fallen at my feet.

Oh, this is the notebook I gave her.

It made me happy to know that she was making use of it.

"Are you okay?" I asked.

I reached out a hand to help her up, but she brushed me off completely.

"Shouldn't you be apologizing for scaring me?" she said.

She stood to her feet, but as soon as she saw the notebook in my hand, her jaw dropped.

"Hm? Oh, yeah," I said. "You're using the notebook, huh? Thanks."

"G-Give it back!"

The red-faced Felm swiped the notebook from my hands.

She's earnestly writing a diary. I guess she really does have a gentle side, so to speak. Maybe she wasn't always a bad kid. Maybe if I approach her the right way, she'll be no different from any other kid her age.

"You didn't read it, did you? Because I'll kill you if you did. I'll murder you."

Well, I guess no different from any other kid her age, besides the threats of murder.

In any case, her magic power was almost entirely sealed in the collar she wore, and my magic was a bad matchup for her anyway.

"You going to eat dinner?" I asked. "You really should. Training on an empty stomach tomorrow will just leave you dry-heaving."

"Eww, don't say that . . . I'll eat."

Something was bothering her, and she left the room with a stony look on her face. It made me chuckle to see her so carefully make sure her diary was in her pocket.

"Well, at least she seems to be making the most of her time here," I said to myself.

It seemed like she was fitting right in with Tong and the others, who at the best of times didn't look human anyway. It didn't seem like we needed to worry about Felm getting into any fights.

As far as training went, she could handle as much as I could, and she was much stronger than Orga. She had a tendency to slack off, but Rose would fix that in time. All that was left was whether or not Kazuki and Inukami-senpai could forgive her. Even though what had happened was in the past, Felm *had* almost killed them, and it wouldn't be easy to forgive her for that.

"How long are you going to just stand there in my room?!" shouted Felm. "Get out!"

"Okay, okay."

This was just the way it was going to be, living under the same roof as Felm.

But I *did* worry how Inukami-senpai would react when she found out.

CHAPTER 5

Usato Goes Searching!

"This will be my first time inside the castle," said Amako, gazing up in awe at the castle as she stood next to me.

I'd picked her up and brought her here first thing in the morning, just like Rose told me to. We greeted the guards at the entrance and went inside, where two maids welcomed us immediately.

"Usato-sama and guest, yes?" said one. "Allow me to take you straight to King Lloyd."

"You're famous, Usato," whispered Amako.

"No need to say it like that," I said with an awkward grin. "I know I don't look the part."

I don't know if I'd ever get used to people calling me "-sama."

We walked down familiar corridors to the hall of the king. The maids ushered us inside, where everyone was waiting: King Lloyd himself, Sergio, Siglis with a big group of knights, Welcie, Kazuki, and Inukami-senpai.

"Good to see you, Usato," said the king.

"And you, Your Majesty," I said.

"And this must be Amako, I presume?"

The king turned his kind eyes on the beastkin girl by my side, who was a little startled in the presence of the king but still managed a nod.

"I see. Well then, now that everyone is here, we can begin. Usato, if you and Amako could stand with Kazuki-sama, please."

"Understood. Come on, Amako. This way."

I gave the girl a gentle pat on the shoulder and her tail shot straight up. She must have been really nervous.

"O-Okay," she said.

Then again, it really was a nerve-wracking experience to meet a nation's ruler. I had just done it so many times now that it no longer fazed me. We walked over to where Kazuki and Inukami-senpai were standing.

"Hi, Usato-kun," said senpai.

"Yo, Usato," added Kazuki.

"I'm glad you two are looking well," I said.

I couldn't put my finger on it exactly, but I felt something had changed in them both over the last ten days. It was only slight, but I wondered if they'd done some kind of special training. It would make sense—they knew as well as I did that we were potentially setting off on a journey.

"The reason I have brought you all here today," said King Lloyd, "is because we have decided once more to reach out to our neighboring nations to request their support. This decision was reached after much discussion with our ministers and military leaders. Our second battle with the Demon Lord's army was comparatively more difficult than the first. The two heroes we brought here to save us were sent to the brink of death, and if not for the Rescue Team, our casualties would be immeasurable."

The king paused a moment with a somber expression to look at everyone gathered. I took a quick glance too, but it was clear that not a single person in attendance disagreed with the man. Rather, everyone looked committed and resolute. I was reminded of just how well-respected King Lloyd was by his people.

He was honest and straightforward, and it was for this reason that many were so loyal. Together, they had built a nation that came to symbolize its leader's personality.

"We must now take action," he said. "We have lived frightened of what stands before us—of the threat of the Demon Lord. Even if we are denied, we must convey this threat to our neighbors in the hope we might unite our forces. The letters to our neighbors will go out in fifteen days, and they will go to the many nations that share our great continent."

Across the whole continent, huh? That probably means we can't send large groups for each letter. But if some of these nations refused to help the first time, they're not going to just jump on board at the arrival of a single letter. We'll have to send someone special.

"For this duty, I elect Suzune, Kazuki . . ."

In other words, we'll have to send heroes.

". . . and Usato. I ask for your help in this matter."

"And that means that I . . ." I muttered, nodding to myself until I realized my name had been announced. "Hang on, what?"

I could understand if it was Inukami-senpai, Kazuki, and Siglis. Nobody would turn those guys down.

Amako looked just as shocked as I did.

"You really *are* famous, Usato," she whispered again.

I was just about to say something when the king spoke again.

"I apologize for always asking such difficult tasks of you, heroes."

"No, we gladly accept this duty," said Kazuki. "The people of Llinger are important to us. It would be our honor."

Inukami-senpai giggled.

"So we get to visit different countries now? Sounds like it'll be tough, but rewarding. Don't you think, Usato-kun?" she said.

"Uh . . . yep. I guess I do."

I wasn't exactly against going, but to be given a role of such importance . . . I had to make sure nobody saw my defeated sigh. Whether the king actually knew how I felt or not, he smiled happily and looked at Amako and me anyway.

"And I apologize to you too, Usato. But there are a few letters going to places that are quite special," he said.

"Special?"

"You will receive a full explanation later. For now, I have said what must be said. We may conclude our meeting here. Suzune, Kazuki, Usato, Amako, Siglis, and Welcie—please remain."

The meeting's attendees left in a line, leaving only the people that the king had requested to stay. King Lloyd watched us for a moment.

Huh? Who are those other three guys? I've never seen them before.

As I looked at the group of three, perplexed, one of them, a girl, winked at me.

Well, that's more friendly than I expected.

"Firstly, Amako," said King Lloyd. "You saved our kingdom from destruction, and for that, you have my gratitude."

The king bowed deeply at the beastkin girl.

Siglis and Welcie were taken completely by surprise, but no one was more shocked than Amako herself.

"Huh?!" she squealed.

"Though I could not do so in front of the crowd earlier, I wish to offer you thanks in person. And for your service, I wish to support you in whatever way I can."

"In that case . . ."

"On Usato's list of places, the last letter will go to the water nation of Mialark."

"That's—!"

"Yes, the city upon water, located in the river that runs through the heart of the continent. On the opposite shores of which lie the Beastlands."

Ah, I see. So that's why the king has decided to send me to this place called Mialark, then. He knew we'd be able to visit the Beastlands as part of our journey.

"However, the path is not an easy one, and I apologize, Usato, but . . ."

"This was a request that I, myself, made," I said. "I take it gladly."

"You have my thanks."

So he said, but really I was the one who should have been thankful.

"As for the countries you will be delivering the letters to . . . Alphie, if you would be so kind as to aid Usato."

The girl named Alphie wore the clothes of a scholar, and her hair was braided.

"As you wish, Your Majesty!" she said. "Usato-sama, Amako-sama, please follow me."

That's the girl who winked at me!

Amako and I bowed to the king and the others, then followed Alphie out of the hall and into a corridor. She walked with a joyous, energetic gait, and she looked very excited as she turned to speak to us.

"This is the first time we've met, I believe. I'm Alphie. I'm a scholar in service to the nation. Well, 'scholar' is a cover-all term for the wide range of research and study I do. Put simply, I gather documentation related to the kingdom's development and I write reports with suggestions for His Majesty. Think of it as knowledge in case of an emergency. I don't mind much if you basically think I'm boring or have too much time on my hands. Anyway, I'd like to give you some information today on the countries you'll be visiting to deliver your letters. It won't be particularly difficult. All the places have roads leading to them, so as long as you're careful about monsters and bandits and that kind of thing, you should be done within a few months."

"Usato," said Amako. "This person talks, like, a *lot.*"

Weird, I was thinking exactly the same thing.

Alphie smiled at Amako, having just given us the entire rundown of what to expect, and then walked off down the corridor.

So this is the person who will teach us all about the geography of the nations that we're delivering letters to.

Alphie led us to a corner of the castle I'd never been to before. She stopped in front of a wooden door in a place without many windows and turned to us with a smile.

"Here we are," she said, pointing at the door. "This is technically my private room, but please come in!"

"Okay," I said.

We walked inside to find a room packed full of piles of paper and stacks of books that almost reached the ceiling. It was amazing. Alphie led the way, brushing aside books and documents as if clearing a path for us. Then she readied a table and some chairs.

Amako and I took a seat, still a little confused, while Alphie rifled through her bookshelf.

"Okay . . . maps, maps, maps . . ." she said, taking a big book from the shelf and brushing the dust from it. "Here we are. Yes, allow me to explain."

Alphie took a big map from the book and opened it on the table.

"This is where we live, the Llinger Kingdom," she explained, "and as you can see, we're the closest nation to the Demon Lord's territory."

Alphie pointed to a location not far from the big green area that must have been the plains where we'd fought not long ago. Around it was a forest and some small villages, but no large nations.

"The area the Demon Lord controls is on the other side of the river, which is on the other side of the plains. The demons crossed that river to get to us."

"Ah, okay . . ." I mumbled.

"Oh, and before I forget: you and the heroes will be going to the same place first."

"Really?"

If we have different letters to send, shouldn't we be taking different routes?

"I know what you're thinking. However, going directly from the kingdom would require you to take some pretty rugged routes, so it's best to take the slightly longer way around. Your actual delivery journeys will start from here: the wizardry city of Luqvist."

Wizardry? I guess that must mean the nation knows its way around magic.

"Now of course, you'll be delivering a letter to Luqvist too. When it comes to magic, Luqvist is where the young compete to be the greatest mages in the whole continent. That said, I'd like you to be careful, Usato—the location is known for harsh discrimination based on magic type. Seeing as you've trained under Rose, we're concerned that you might punch, kick, or throw some of the students all over the place."

Alphie giggled mischievously. Amako joined her. I didn't think it was funny in the slightest.

"Talk about hitting a guy where it hurts. I'm not that kind of monster," I said.

"I thought it was *very* funny," Amako said.

Such a wide grin. Does she think I'm a joke?

I'm a human. I'm not like Rose. *I'm not strong enough to send people flying like pinballs. I'm not so beastly I'll wake up the unconscious and force them to go jogging.*

It was weird to me that people would think me and Rose were the same just because we were both on the Rescue Team.

"The fact you can call Rose a monster means you are exactly the sort of person I've heard about. In any case, after your trip to Luqvist, you'll have to deliver three more letters," Alphie went on.

"So including the Beastlands, that makes four?" I asked.

"No, I've included the Beastlands. Your end goal is Mialark, which is here."

Alphie pointed to a huge circular shape in a massive river, which had the stamp of a country on it.

Wow, that's a long way from Llinger Kingdom.

"You'll deliver a letter to the queen here, as well as delivering a letter to the Prayerlands of Samariarl."

"Samariarl . . ."

Amako trembled at the mere mention of the name, and her tail stood on end.

Did something happen there? I have a bad feeling about this.

"It's the country most likely to offer us their support, but they don't take very kindly to demi-humans."

"Heavily discriminatory, you mean?" I asked.

"That's correct. So upon entering this country, Amako, you'll have to be very careful. You should be fine in the country itself, but Usato, I don't think it's wise to take her for your audience with the king. I know it's going to be uncomfortable, but the heroes are going in a completely different direction from the Beastlands."

"You don't have to apologize," I said. "I'm happy you're helping us."

The Prayerlands, huh? Sounds like they might be fervently religious. I hope we'll be okay. I don't really believe in God much myself, so I doubt I'll be affected. Still, if the king of the place is anti-demi-human to the nth degree and he finds out about Amako, we could be looking at big trouble.

"This is way less than I expected," I said. "Just three letters? Really?"

"We can't afford to spend too much time on this task," she went on. "We've entrusted the appropriate knights with delivering letters to other countries. The heroes and you are delivering letters to the nations that are uniquely challenging—they are not likely to easily offer their services. However, if we are not successful in convincing them, fighting the Demon Lord may well prove impossible."

I had no words.

"That is why the Llinger Kingdom is sending our nation's most powerful—the heroes, and you. We intend to show them we are determined, resolute, and honest in our request for support."

Pressure, much? This responsibility weighs a ton.

"I don't know how much of that I can show them just by visiting their home," I said.

"That depends largely on you and your actions. Though you may not have noticed, here in the kingdom, everyone knows who you are. The Rescue Team has saved countless lives. Don't you think it's likely that stories of your efforts have reached these other nations? Whether they believe them, however, is another thing entirely."

"I'm not all that thrilled to be famous, honestly," I stated.

My shoulders drooped and I let out a sigh.

I sure hope those stories haven't wandered off into the unbelievable. But I guess I'll cross that *bridge when I get to it.*

"Now, as for the Beastlands . . . unfortunately, our knowledge of the place is still very limited. All we know for certain is that you get there by boat from Mialark."

"That's fine," said Amako. "I can explain the rest to Usato."

"Well then, that's a relief," replied Alphie. "The country keeps itself closed off from others, and our only documents are very old."

That wasn't particularly surprising. We were talking about a country of people that had been discriminated against, hated, and suffered terribly as a result. Why would they even *want* to be friendly? Relations were bound to be poor.

"How big will our traveling party be?" I asked.

"We'd like to keep things small scale, so we're thinking around five. It might be better for you to travel with less, Usato—you're used to running in and around battlefields, so it may be harder for you if the group is too large and unwieldy."

"Well, uh . . . I guess so . . ." I stuttered.

But actually, she'd nailed it. It was like she could read my thoughts.

"I've already mentioned that you'll be traveling with the heroes, but your final destination—the Beastlands—is an especially sensitive location. In recent years there have been problems regarding slavery and discrimination. If Amako is seen in the company of battle-hardened heroes, they may be attacked on sight. With that in mind, it would be best to focus the party on you, with only one or two knights as accompaniment."

"I'll be fine as long as I have people with me who have enough common sense and knowledge," I said. "But I can see how muscling into the Beastlands with a large group would put everyone on edge."

Amako nodded in agreement. It seemed we were approaching things from the right direction.

That leaves the question of who to bring along with us. Ideally someone who can stand up to bandits and danger along the way. Ah-ha. Now **there's** *someone we can trust.*

"Uh . . . about our traveling partners. How about Aruku?" I asked.

"Aruku . . . Ah! You mean the guard! I see, I see. And he *is* more worldly than he appears. . . Yes. You've got sharp eyes, Usato-sama!" Alphie exclaimed.

The red-haired Aruku wasn't just cool and a good guard; he could handle himself around danger too, and he was trustworthy—he'd been essential to the protection of the Rescue Team in our last battle.

That, and he was smart.

"Once we're done here, I'll talk to him. I'm sure he'd be happy to help. Well, I think that's everything I needed to explain . . . Oh, I almost forgot. I need to tell you about what happens *after* you visit the Beastlands."

"Afterwards? Oh, right, because we still have to come home once we're done," I said.

I'd been too wrapped up in thoughts of just getting to our destination.

"Coming home should be rather straightforward and simple. You'll come back here by way of Luqvist. Delivering the letter there on your way back is also an option, but we'd prefer not to put that burden on you."

"I guess the route home is going to be pretty uneventful then," I muttered.

At the very least, it seems like coming back will be . . . easier? That said, we still don't have any idea how successful we'll be at actually seeing our duties through.

With our discussion complete, Alphie excused herself to head to King Lloyd to deliver her report. She said we were done for the day and could return home, so that was exactly what we decided to do.

I would have liked to talk with Inukami-senpai and Kazuki, but I figured they had their own journeys to think about, so I decided to save that for another day. And besides, we wouldn't be departing for another two weeks, so there was plenty of time.

"Well, let's head home, Amako. I'll walk you to your house."

"Thanks."

I matched Amako's pace and we started walking. Our destinations were now official—we'd deliver three letters and help Amako's mother.

"So first up, we're heading to Luqvist," I said. "I wonder what kind of place it is."

"I've been there before."

"Oh, really? What sort of place is it?"

No harm in having a little foreknowledge before we get there.

Amako stopped for a moment at my question, then took off walking again.

"There's a school where they teach magic, and there are more kids than there are adults."

Wow, more kids, huh? As soon as I heard the word "mage," I figured it would be a bunch of grandpas researching magic. I'd imagined old men with long beards silently rummaging through books and studying various magic. But when I heard about the kids, I wondered if it worked as a place to raise and educate young people about my age.

"I'm guessing that because it's a place of wizardry, there are lots of people who know magic, right?" I asked.

"Right. People come from across the continent, and there are mages of all different magical types. That, and . . ." Amako stopped for a moment and pointed at my face. "There's a healer there too."

"Oh, so there's one in Luqvist, huh?"

A healer that didn't belong to the Rescue Team.

I wonder what sort of person this healer is? Maybe the healer uses a different healing magic than Rose and me. At least it's one more thing to look forward to!

"I wouldn't get too excited," said Amako. "Healing magic isn't valued very highly there, so it's probably not what you're imagining."

And it *was* true that healers only had access to healing—a magic that lacked any kind of skill. That, and first aid magic was a general magic spell already used in emergencies. Why even bother relying on healing magic when there was a simpler magic available? Maybe in Luqvist, healers were ashamed of their magic.

"You were looking for healers before, right? Does that mean you met the healer in Luqvist?" I asked.

"Yes. We talked in my precognitive vision."

That didn't make things sound very promising. I prodded Amako a little, and after some hesitation, she opened up.

"When I talked to him in my precognitive vision, I knew right away . . ."

"You knew what?"

"He couldn't help me, and I couldn't help him. What he's wrapped up in is not an easy matter to solve, and he no longer trusts anyone."

I wonder if that's why she told me not to get excited.

Whatever the case, I decided I probably shouldn't pry any further.

"Well, thanks for the info, anyway," I said. "Let's get going."

"Okay."

The healer of Luqvist sounded like he came with some baggage, but all the same, I wanted to meet him. First, however, I had to report to Rose.

* * *

". . . and that's everything," I said.

"Hm."

After seeing Amako home safe, I returned to the training grounds, where Rose was watching over Felm's training.

"They've got you going to some really troublesome places, huh?" she said. "Meh. You'll be fine."

"You sound awfully optimistic."

"Do I?" said Rose, grinning. "Why? You worried?"

I let out a defeated sigh.

"Well, not as worried as when I first came here and had to go through training with you."

"Ha! Well said."

Underneath Rose and her cackling, Felm was struggling through push-ups.

"Ex . . . Excuse me . . . I . . . exist, you know . . ." she muttered.

I scratched my cheek as I watched her. It brought back memories of when I first came here. I felt myself getting all nostalgic.

"Keep at it," I said. "It was harsher than this when I went through it."

"Huh?!" Felm spat. "If *you* did it, then I am more than capable of doing it!"

She gritted her teeth and she pushed herself through more push-ups. Rose ran a hand through her hair, unimpressed.

"I'll be taking her to the forest soon, so look after the place while I'm gone," she said.

"Bit early, don't you think?" I asked.

"This one's always trying to make things easy on herself. Gonna have to take her somewhere where she can't and knock that bad habit out of her."

So the monster's going to force the laziness from Felm's personality, huh?

"I guess however long it takes, it's something everyone goes through," I said.

"Your time was special. This one doesn't have enough guts, so I'm going to leave her there right until the limit."

Felm was so focused on her push-ups that she couldn't hear us, so she didn't know that come tomorrow, she would know true hell. But I was at least relieved to know she wouldn't have to go through quite as awful of an experience as I went through . . . probably.

Felm let out a series of strange grunts. She'd overworked herself and she crumpled to the ground. Rose had gone from sitting in a chair to sitting on a mattress.

"Tch. Again?!" she shouted. "How many times now?! Get up! Now you have to do another five hundred, you useless loafer!"

Felm groaned something unintelligible.

"No matter how many times she does it, she always goes too far," Rose said, standing up. Then, while Felm's shoulders were still trembling, Rose sent healing magic to Felm's feet and kicked the girl, shouting at her the whole time.

I expected tears to follow soon, so I silently left the training grounds. I didn't want to get pulled into it. I didn't mind going along with training, but Felm might end up so sad she'd curse me for the rest of her life. But as soon as I heard the weeping, I had a feeling she already felt that way.

"Keep at it," I muttered, though my words would never reach her.

* * *

The next day, as I was feeding Blurin at the stables, I heard a now familiar female scream. Blurin and I both left the stables. We had a feeling we knew what to expect, and sure enough, Rose was leaving the dorms with a large rucksack on her back and an unconscious Felm on her shoulders.

To anyone who didn't know any better, it was quite the unusual sight.

Suddenly, I heard a high-pitched squeal and felt something climbing up to my shoulders. I turned to find a furry black creature with red eyes.

Ah, you must be what Rose was looking for.

"The captain's calling you, Kukuru," I said.

So just like when I was in the forest, Kukuru was going to pretend to help Felm out too. The rabbit actually *did* help me out with its sensor-like abilities, but a kind of disgust welled up in me when I thought about how the friendship I'd felt in that forest was little more than an act.

Still, I guess the fact that Kukuru was on my shoulder now meant that it had grown used to me. I gave it a pat as it cleaned its fur, then it leaped from my shoulder with stunning speed and ran to Rose's feet before scrambling to her shoulder.

"Won't be back for a while," Rose said, looking at me. "Be good."

Her glare sent a shiver down my spine that had me speaking with excessive politeness.

"Understood! Please have a safe trip!"

Satisfied with my reply, Rose, Kukuru, and the unconscious Felm made their way to the gates. Blurin growled in a way that said, *Hurry up and feed me, dolt!* Then Blurin slapped me on the leg.

Oh, that's right. I was right in the middle of feeding you.

"Is this what you want, you glutton?"

I held out the fruit in my hand and the grizzly ate it hungrily. I remembered that I used to worry about the bear eating my fingers off along with the food I gave him. But surprisingly, it never happened. As a matter of habit, grizzlies weren't messy eaters, and Blurin was quite neat when he came to eating what I gave him.

"Well, what should we do now that the captain is gone?" I asked.

I thought about the time I had left before we departed—fourteen days, including today. Usually, I'd train and make sure I was in top shape, but . . . I didn't think it would have a huge impact. I could always work out while we were on the road anyway.

That made me wonder, what could I do here that I couldn't do anywhere else?

Study?

I'd already read the entire book that Rose gave me, so studying wasn't super important.

Fighting skills? Sword work?

I didn't have any battle experience outside of using my fists and feet, but I didn't think there was a lot I could pick up in the space of ten or so days. Still, it wouldn't hurt to get my feet wet when it came to battle tactics, so I decided to keep that in mind.

"I guess that leaves . . . healing magic?"

When I thought about it more deeply, I realized that I only knew the basics of healing magic. All I had was a vague understanding of how to heal injuries, exhaustion, and illnesses.

So how about deepening your knowledge of healing magic while Rose is away?

It was a solid idea, and better still, there were excellent healers just as good as Rose right here in the Llinger Kingdom.

"Let's head off once we're done with training," I said.

Blurin growled a complaint in response.

"Oh, sorry. Food, right."

I held out another fruit for Blurin as my thoughts whirled with what I could do with the fourteen days before departure. Orga was easily as good a healer as Rose, and he must know stuff he could teach me.

So I decided I'd finish training a little earlier than usual and visit the infirmary!

* * *

"Where are you going, Lady Suzune?" asked Aruku, who was guarding the castle gates.

"Hm? Oh, just to the Rescue Team base."

The sun was high in the sky and it was time I took a break, so I was heading to see Usato at the Rescue Team headquarters. Aruku caught me as I was leaving.

"You're going to see Sir Usato?!"

I felt a little overwhelmed by the admiration and politeness I heard in his tone.

"Um, yes." I nodded.

Aruku was assigned to defend the castle gates and was extremely important to maintaining a high level of protection. Even Siglis thought highly of the guy. Some thought he was a bit weird though, having turned down squad captain and imperial guard positions and *requested* to be put on castle gate protection.

Then again, if that weren't the case, he never would have been chosen to go with me for my training outside of the castle. Back then, Usato and I had gone missing because of my slip-up. Aruku had devoted himself to searching for us, even at the cost of his own rest. I knew right then exactly how upstanding and loyal the guy was.

"I saw him heading for town just a short while ago," said Aruku.

"Town? Alright, I guess I'll head that way then," I replied.

I wanted to ask him about the School of Magic, which was located in the Wizardry City of Luqvist. We were in another world, so I had super high hopes for the place. I was very excited. I had to let it out somewhere.

"Oh, by the way, do you know much about Luqvist, Aruku?" I asked.

"I do. It's, well . . . It's hard to call it a *good* place per se, but there's no better place for learning magic."

"Wait, so you're saying . . ."

"Yes, I learned magic there for a time. That's all I have, really—my blade and my magic. I'm practically useless when it comes to anything else," Aruku said with a bright chuckle.

But from what I could see, Aruku was quite strong. I'd heard he could wield fire magic and that his sword work was nothing to balk at. Two knights near Aruku seemed to read my thoughts, and they crossed their arms and nodded in agreement.

"Aruku," said one, "all you have trouble with is the staff and the bow, no? Lady Suzune, believe me when I tell you that this guy could be an imperial guard if he so desired."

"He's not joking," said the other. "None of us can work out why this guy doesn't want to make more coin."

Aruku was momentarily shaken by the sudden comments but quickly regained his composure.

"You guys . . ." he muttered.

"Hm? What are they talking about exactly?" I asked, prodding.

Aruku tried to wave me off with a wry chuckle, but when that didn't work, he sighed and scratched the back of his head.

"Well," he said, a bit embarrassed, "I can't defend more than one thing because I'm pretty uncoordinated."

"But even then, you could still be a member of the imperial guard, no?" I said.

The imperial guard was tasked with protecting the king. Was Aruku saying he couldn't do that?

"No, the imperial guards must be flexible—the king is their priority, but they have to be ready to protect others as the situation calls for it. It's a little too much for me, so I protect the castle."

He turned to look at it. It was surrounded by tough, durable walls that stood tall and denied trespassers.

"So long as I do my job here, no intruders get in, so nobody in the castle gets hurt. But it's all over if someone can make it past me and through the gates!"

Aruku said it with a joking smile, but secretly, it gave me goosebumps.

This guy's got hot-blooded main-character qualities! Not to mention he's good-looking—but in a different way than Kazuki.

"But I'm going to have to leave the protection of the castle to my fellow knights for a little while," said Aruku.

"Hm? And why's that?" I asked, head tilted with curiosity.

Aruku quickly stood to attention with his legs together, his back straight, and a fist on his chest.

"I, the knight Aruku," he said, proudly, "have been selected to assist Sir Usato of the Rescue Team on his journey!"

"Huh?" I said, sounding like a surprised dolt.

Aruku laughed.

"I was as surprised as you are. I only found out about it yesterday, from one of the castle attendants."

I can't believe he already selected a knight to accompany him. But then I should expect nothing less of Usato-kun. He's got a sharp eye. But I have to say I can't believe that he so casually chose someone so formidable. That means Usato-kun saw it too . . . He saw Aruku's main-character qualities.

I giggled.

"I have no choice but to admit defeat, Usato-kun," I muttered. "Well, you take good care of Usato-kun, okay, Aruku?"

"Of course!"

And so I headed into town, haunted by the feeling of complete and utter defeat.

Usato-kun should be fine if he's traveling with Aruku. He can outrun all but the most ferocious of foes. And things will only be safer if he's traveling with a prescient like Amako. A party like that is totally OP. Like, how do you even stop them?

"Which means . . ."

I'm the one with a problem.

I was heading to the country of Kamelio, which fervently worshiped the heroes. It wasn't particularly far, but it looked like it would be a handful.

Because we'll be way too popular!

"No, I can't let myself get disheartened."

On the bright side, Kamelio's cooperation was almost guaranteed so long as Kazuki and I visited, which meant we had to go.

Still, just hearing about it put a weight in the pit of my stomach.

* * *

With my morning training done, I headed into town to go to the infirmary alone. When people saw me in town now, they didn't kick up quite the stir they used to. Still, I could always feel people watching me.

Then again, until now they'd always seen me running down the street with a grizzly in my arms, so they weren't about to change overnight.

I opened the door to the infirmary and headed inside.

"Hello?" I said, announcing myself.

The infirmary hadn't changed since the last time I was here.

It was as clean as the Rescue Team base. Coming back filled me with the deep feelings I held for the place.

"Coming!" I heard Ururu's voice from the back of the infirmary, and in a few moments, she came running. "Oh, hey there, Usato-kun," she said.

"Hey, Ururu. I came to see Orga today. Is he busy?"

"I don't think so. It's a good day here today—no patients."

A good day, huh?

But the words rang true. If there were no patients, there would be no injuries or illnesses to worry about.

With that in mind, yeah. It **is** *a good day.*

I followed the grinning Ururu as I explained to her why I'd come.

"Oh, I see. So you want to learn more about Orga's healing magic . . . Sure, I think it's a great idea. That's about all he's good for, anyway!"

Wow, that's kind of harsh. Maybe spitting poison is her natural state.

"By the way, I heard all about the training you got wrapped up in. Sparring with Rose? That's crazy!"

"What? That's not what it was."

How did the truth turn into that*?*

"Oh, it wasn't?" Ururu laughed. "Oh, right. Of course not. If you sparred with Rose . . ."

"It wasn't sparring," I said, "because I wasn't allowed to hit her back."

". . . she would kill you . . . Huh?"

I mean, it didn't really matter what I tried. It would have been a one-sided beating anyway. So I just covered up like a turtle and tried to dodge and weave the best I could.

"I gave it everything I had," I said, "but I think the captain was going kind of easy on me. I mean, look at me—I'm still alive. But anyway, where did that sparring rumor come from?"

Ururu laughed again.

"It seems some kids heard the noises coming from the training ground and decided to go check it out. They ran away crying and said that you and Rose got in a fight."

So that's how it started. Maybe they saw me practically pleading for my own life. I had a feeling I'd been doing that. Come to think of it, I still was.

"Whatever you guys were up to, it sounded rough. Well," said Ururu, stopping in front of a door. "This is Orga's room."

"Thanks."

"Usato-kun is here," shouted Ururu, knocking on the door.

"Come in," said an exhausted voice from behind it.

We walked inside to find Orga sitting at a desk in the corner of a simple room.

"Sorry to barge in on you so soon after your recovery, Orga," I said.

"I don't mind. Seeing people is one of life's small joys."

This was Ururu's brother, Orga Fleur, a healer as powerful as Rose and the head of the infirmary.

The person I would be asking to teach me about healing magic.

"I see," said Orga after I explained why I came, "so you want to learn more healing magic before you leave on your journey."

Orga nodded and dropped into thought for a time. I didn't get the feeling he was about to turn me away.

"But all the same," he said, "I don't think it's necessary for you to learn anything from me. I'm certain you could become a more powerful healer than me in no time."

"Still, while the captain is away," I pleaded, "I'd like to use this time to learn from you!"

Orga crossed his arms, and a troubled look spread across his face. Ururu gave him a light punch.

"Okay, okay," she said, "how about we compare our healing magic? At least then we can probably work out how his healing magic differs from our own. That sound okay to you, Usato-kun?"

"Fine by me," I said.

"Okay, let's do it!" she exclaimed.

"I see you're not asking *my* opinion," said Orga with a chuckle.

Orga held his hand out, and I did the same. Ururu smiled at me as I released healing magic into my hand. The color of it was the same light shade of green as when I'd touched the crystal upon being summoned here. Ururu's healing magic was a slightly darker shade than my own. But Orga's . . .

"Just as I thought," I said.

Orga's magic was a deep, dense green.

Though it was still transparent, it was a dark green like fresh leaves. When I thought about it, Rose's healing magic was darker than my own, but not as dark as Orga's.

"How do you cast your magic, Orga?" I asked. "I don't think of anything special when I create this, and this color is the result."

"Same as me," Orga replied. "My magic is slightly different to yours and Ururu's, but it was something I was born with."

"You were born with it?" I said.

"My magic is very good at healing the illnesses of others. However, I am not very good at healing myself. It's quite pitiful, I know," he said, chuckling.

Does that mean the color of the magic dictates its healing level?

I looked at the magic in my hand and slowly clenched my fist. It was the same light as when I always cast it. It was the same green as the day that I arrived in this world.

"As far as I know," said Orga, "healing an illness with healing magic is different than simply healing an external injury in a number of ways. You're healing *inside* of the body. Does that make sense? Think of it this way, Usato-kun—you're not *mending;* you're *healing.*"

"I . . . don't really get it," said Ururu, "but are you saying that your healing magic is a step beyond our own, Orga?"

"I suppose that's one way to think about it, yes."

Orga's magic is a step beyond my own. Perhaps Rose knows something more about it. Still, I have a feeling it's something I have to do myself. Basically, if my healing magic is light in color now, then making it darker will change its properties. And if I make my healing magic the same color as Orga's, then I'll be able to heal the same illnesses, right?

"Wonder if I can force it . . ." I said.

I tried pouring in more magic without making it bigger. The healing magic covered my hand, and I began pouring more in. My hypothesis was that I could raise the density of the magic. I felt my magic spurting from my hand like electricity.

"Usato-kun, what are you doing?"

"Hm? Oh, I'm just pouring more magic power into my hand."

I kept my eyes on my hand the whole time, and as the magic poured in, the surface of the magic on my hand began to deepen in color.

I can do it.

But no sooner had the thought left my mind than Orga let out a gasp and grabbed my arm.

"Usato-kun! Stop that at once!"

"Huh?"

Even though I'm so close?

That was what I was about to say, but right then, the magic pouring into my hand glowed and then . . . burst.

* * *

"I'm sorry to cause you all that trouble, Orga," I said, bowing apologetically as I left the infirmary.

"Don't worry about any of that," replied Orga, who saw me off at the door with a worried look on his face. "But please refrain from doing what you tried earlier. Ururu is just as worried."

I looked at my hand as I walked the town's bustling main street and let out a sigh. It had been about an hour since I'd funneled magic into my hand. When I did it, my hand really was wrapped in a darker shade of healing magic. But in the next instant, it was like my hand couldn't bear the magic power accumulating in it, which made it burst.

Well, I say "burst," but it wasn't like it exploded. It was more like fissures opened up on my hand and my magic started pouring from them. It wasn't as bad an injury as it looked at the time.

But what surprised me when it happened was that my healing magic didn't work the way it was supposed to. All the same, at least I could eventually heal my hand back to normal afterward. According to Orga, what I had just tried was something very dangerous.

Still, I'd come away with a new understanding. It was like a rule had revealed itself to me.

"The scope of a healing magic changes based on its density," I said out loud.

I'd also learned one more thing: the darker the color of a healing magic, the harder it became to self-heal. When my hand had burst, I hadn't been able to heal it with the darker-colored healing magic I'd made. Now I could understand why Orga, who was born with a denser healing magic, had so much trouble healing his own wounds.

"It's totally worth working on though," I muttered.

If I did it a few times, I had a feeling I could get the hang of it. And if I could raise the density of my magic power, I'd be able to heal people just as quickly as Orga and Rose did. This would make it easier to heal the people I currently had difficulty healing.

But to get to that level . . .

"Practice makes perfect, I guess," I surmised.

I gathered healing light in my right hand to deepen its color. The great thing about this particular kind of training was that I could do it pretty much anywhere.

"Usato-kun!"

I heard a voice behind me and spun toward it.

"Hm? Oh, Inukami-senpai."

She waved at me and ran over with a bright grin on her face. She seemed more excited than usual.

"I know this is kind of sudden," she said, "but how did you see Aruku's main-character potential?!"

"Seriously, what are you even talking about?"

She wasn't kidding when she said "sudden."

I was going to go back to the training grounds to work on my magic, but now that I'd bumped into Inukami-senpai, I figured I'd hang out a bit more.

"One second," I said. I inhaled deeply to prepare myself, then exhaled long and determined. "Alright, I'm good."

"Wait a second. Why the long breath? Is talking to me *that* annoying, Usato-kun?"

I laughed it off.

"Of course not."

"So why won't you look me in the eyes?!"

Because a part of me thinks it is *that annoying.*

But it wasn't like I was about to tell her that to her face.

CHAPTER 6

The Journey Begins!

Rose and Felm returned from the forest. I think maybe they were gone for about ten days. It was about the same amount of time that I was gone.

Upon her return, Felm looked tired of the whole world. I could hear it in the hollow sound of her voice as she muttered about "betrayal." It made me think she'd had the same black rabbit experience that I had. That said, she seemed mentally tougher too. But that was just a feeling, so I couldn't say anything for certain.

A few things had happened while Rose and Felm were gone.

Firstly, the king's plan to send letters to various nations was announced to the public. This announcement followed the same routine as when he announced the battle with the Demon Lord's army, so there were no big changes there. Also, Aruku visited to tell me he'd be joining me on my journey. As he was heading back to the castle, I told him I wanted to keep our party small—because our group would be less agile if it was too large—but I wasn't sure if that was how things would work out.

"Hm . . ." I muttered, lost in thought as I cast healing magic into my hand.

Other than the announcement and Aruku, I'd just been working on my healing magic while Rose was away. In terms of results, I hadn't gotten very far. It was difficult to make the magic denser in the first place, and then, on top of that, I couldn't maintain the magic power. What it came down to was instinct—I had to keep the density level consistent *and* keep my magic power stable. It was really hard. I could hold it for a few seconds, but as soon as my focus slipped, the magic dissipated.

"Damn, this is difficult," I grumbled.

I was at the training grounds, sitting on one of the rocks we used for training weights. I kept working on focusing my magic, but I just couldn't keep it stable. It really bothered me that I still didn't have anything to show for my efforts, especially because we were leaving tomorrow. Until now, I'd been able to see my results thanks to Rose's training: it was in my improved endurance and ability to use healing magic. The training was as hard as nails, but I got out what I put into it, and all of it had gotten me this far.

"Guess not everything is so straightforward," I grumbled some more.

I stayed there, cross-legged on that rock, and tried to make my magic denser again. But just like before, it just dissipated into the air, probably because I wasn't focused enough.

I guess ten days just isn't enough time to master something like this.

"Hey, Usato."

"Huh?!" I said, almost jumping off the rock because of Rose's sudden, soundless appearance. "Oh, Captain. Something wrong?"

"Just now, what was that?"

"Hm?"

Huh? What is this? She's confused?

I'd never seen Rose look like that before. She grabbed the hand I was pouring my magic power into.

"When did you learn to boost your own magic?"

"S-Sorry! Am I not supposed to be doing that?!"

"Answer me."

What? Did I do something I wasn't supposed to? Then again, Orga got angry too. Maybe it really **is** *dangerous.*

I was still scared of Rose's potential reaction, but all the same, I explained the training I'd been doing.

"It's because I saw Orga's healing magic," I said. "I've just been trying to see if I can deepen my own magic power too."

"Orga? So you saw his magic, and you tried to do this?"

Rose released my hand and crossed her arms. She watched me as she fell into thought. After a few seconds of silence, her mouth curled into a grin, she covered her eyes, and then she started to laugh softly. It was honestly terrifying to see this woman laughing.

"Um, is something wrong?" I asked.

Has she finally gone insane?

The rude thought fluttered through my mind as Rose's laughter faded and she placed a hand on my head and smiled at me. Her smile, too, was petrifying. I'd never seen anything like it. I found myself instinctively freeing my hands so that I would be ready for whatever pain was about to come next. However, Rose simply ruffled my hair with a satisfied grin on her face.

"That's a unique characteristic of healing magic," she said. "You've probably noticed already, but when the color gets darker, your external healing magic is strengthened but your internal healing magic weakens."

"Ah, so it's just as I thought, then," I said.

"I thought the ability was still beyond you. Use it the wrong way and the result can be death. But it's not like I can stop you now that you've started it. It's not easy, but you can master it with practice." Rose chuckled. "Never would have thought you'd work it out on your own though. You surprise even me sometimes."

So that means it's only natural I still don't have control of it now. The training is **supposed** *to take a long time. Now that I know that, I'm ready to keep at it.*

"Is there any, I don't know, knack to this?" I asked.

"Practice," said Rose, "and lots of it. There are no short-cuts. It's just like everything else you've done until now. But you managed to master the other skills, so you can master this one too."

So there's no way to get any better than to just put in the time and the reps. I guess I'll just keep on practicing the way I have been. I can still get stronger.

I clenched my fist, knowing now that there were still ways for me to keep pushing onward.

"Oh, I forgot to tell you something," said Rose. "I know your letter delivery journey starts tomorrow, and the kingdom's attendants told me what time you'll be leaving. I know you're not much for big send-offs, so just get to the gates first thing in the morning, and take Amako with you."

"Oh, okay. Got it."

"The heroes' traveling party will be along in time, so you can just meet them there."

I guessed that Rose was talking about the kingdom's people sending off the heroes. I could see them riding a carriage through the city streets, surrounded by shouts and cheers . . . which, as Rose knew, wasn't my thing at all, even if it was expected of senpai and Kazuki.

"What about luggage?" I asked.

"Take your uniform and your casual clothes. Other than that, the bare essentials should be fine. If you're taking the grizzly with you, then he can carry some stuff for you too. All you need is some rope to tie it on with."

Just the bare essentials, huh? I guess that means the book Rose gave me, my knife, my notebook, and some field rations.

"Any other questions?" she asked.

"Not right now, no."

"In that case, there's one thing you should know before you leave."

"What's that?"

I thought she would give me some advice for a world full of unknown dangers. She was usually on the money when it came to that sort of thing, so I listened carefully as Rose clenched a fist and raised it, grinning.

"If you ever find yourself with worthless scum who look down on healing magic, you send them flying. Don't even think twice."

"I can't just do that! I'll get into all sorts of trouble!" I shouted.

Talk about sadistic advice!

"Some people, they're so pathetic they only know how to judge things on a surface level. Smacking some sense into them is the right thing to do," she told me.

"Uh . . . Oh . . . kay . . ." I stuttered.

For now, I took her kind words along with the dangerous ones. I had no idea where this woman's boiling point was, so I never had any idea when and what she was going to do.

That was my captain, alright.

"I think that's everything," she said finally. "Now go and get ready. You'll want to be done before dark."

"Got it."

"I'm heading back. However your journey goes, you'll come out of it with something. I'm counting on you, Usato."

And with that, Rose left the training grounds. I watched her go and thought about what she'd said.

"She's counting on me," I said, repeating her words to myself. "Dammit, that sure makes me happy."

It surprised me, how simple I was at heart.

But perhaps what makes me really *happy is that it's Rose doing the complimenting. Probably. I might do my share of bitching and moaning, but I trust and believe in her.*

And as my teacher in this world, I respect her.

"Well, now that I know what I need to know, better get packing," I muttered.

I still had to make a leather belt for Blurin, among other things. I stretched and started walking back to the Rescue Team headquarters when I noticed someone in the shade of a tree by the training grounds.

"Felm?" I said, stopping. "What are you doing?"

The demon girl sounded a little startled that I noticed her, but then she stormed out looking angrier than I'd seen her before. She dropped her gaze away from my eyes.

"I'm not allowed to go to town even when I get time off, so I'm going for a walk . . . That's when I saw you," she stated.

Even though she's changed and she's calmer now, she was Llinger's enemy not so long ago. I can see why she's not allowed into town, no matter how tolerant and accepting the people of Llinger are.

"Oh, okay," I said. "But why were you hiding?"

"B-Because I hate you."

I wonder why she hates me so much. Oh, wait. No, that makes perfect sense. I **did** *beat the crap out of her. Then again, guess there's not much I can do about how she feels. And besides, I have to get ready for tomorrow.*

"It's not often we get breaks, so make sure you rest up," I said.

I went to walk past Felm, but she suddenly grabbed ahold of my arm.

"Wait," she said.

"Hm?"

"Where are you going tomorrow?"

"Oh. Come to think of it, I didn't tell you."

"So tell me now."

"Huh?"

"I said tell me now!" Felm demanded, drawing closer to me.

First, she hates me. Then she wants to talk to me. What a girl.

I gave Felm a quick explanation of the journey I was heading out on. She seemed to flare up with anger for a moment and I thought she was going to push even closer to me, but then she looked down at her feet.

"What's wrong?" I asked. "Wait, don't tell me you're going to be lone—"

Felm kicked me in the shin. I don't know why. She just did that when she was unhappy about something. I was used to that kind of pain, so I never showed it on my face. But she *was* a demon, and she *did* have all their strength, which is why I think my shin went numb.

I was just joking, but maybe she will be lonely.

Felm grunted.

"Wait, are you *really* going to be—"

"It's not fair that only you get to escape this hellhole of a place!"

"Oh. *Oh*, okay. *That's* what you mean."

Felm looked at me for an instant, then kicked me in the shin again and took off running in the opposite direction. She kicked me pretty hard that second time, and I felt my anger flare up.

When I get angry, I get **angry**, *you know . . .*

"Wait, wait. Calm down, Usato."

I was almost thinking like Rose for a second there.

Still, I had more experience here than Felm did, so I cooled my temper and watched her jog away into the distance.

I think it might be best just to let her go. I'm not going to be able to change her, what with me heading off on my own journey tomorrow. But what did she mean by "hellhole," anyway?

I let out a sigh.

Never mind. Today we'll just forgive and forget.

I felt a little like I'd grown up, and I headed back toward the Rescue Team lodgings to get ready.

* * *

On the morning of our departure, I woke up especially early and went to the fruit shop where Amako lived.

"Don't worry, you'll get used to it in no time," I said to Blurin. "You just have to give it a little time."

I stood out in my bright white Rescue Team uniform with my backpack filled with necessities, but the growling grizzly by my side stood out even more. I'd wrapped a belt around Blurin so I could secure baggage to him. Fortunately, it didn't impede his movements—and I was still carrying most of our stuff—but the bear still wasn't particularly happy to be wearing something he wasn't used to.

I chuckled and gave him a pat on the nose. I looked over at the fruit shop where Amako and a woman were just coming out. The woman said a few words to Amako that I couldn't make out from where I was standing, and then she wrapped the beastkin girl in a hug. At first, Amako seemed surprised, but then she looked down, her tail and her shoulders trembling.

This must be a really hard moment for Amako and that woman.

I didn't want to get in the way of something that was clearly important to both of them, so I kept my distance and just watched. When the woman let Amako go, she looked at me and bowed deeply.

I felt a message in her gesture:

"*Please take care of Amako.*"

She had looked after Amako, and now it was up to me to take on that responsibility.

"It's kind of heavy," I muttered to myself as Amako walked over to us.

I wasn't sure what to say to her, and I hated myself for it. As I scrambled for something to say, Amako took my sleeve and pulled on it.

"You don't have to say anything," Amako said. "But . . . thank you."

She'd seen a few seconds into the future, and she smiled up at the dumbfounded look on my face. Seeing her like that, I let out a relieved sigh. We started walking to the meeting point.

"Usato," said Amako.

"What is it?" I asked, walking in time with her little steps.

"Do you think it would be okay for me to come back here?"

What does she mean by that? Does she not intend to come back to the Llinger Kingdom? Or does she mean that she won't be able to?

I tilted my head curiously as Amako looked at the ground.

"She said that I could come back whenever I wanted . . ." muttered Amako. "She said I would always have a home here . . ."

"The woman said that to you?"

"Yes, but I don't know if I'll be able to come back. I might never be able to come back ever again."

Rose **had** *called her a time-reading princess, after all.*

And perhaps that was what Amako was talking about. Perhaps she was much more important than I had ever thought. And when I thought about that, I felt unable to say anything to her as she stared at the ground. I did not know what burdens she had to bear, and as such, I did not know what words would ease her worries.

"Some help I am . . ." I muttered to myself, picking up my pace as the gates appeared in the distance.

About an hour after Amako and I arrived at the gate, we heard loud voices coming from town and saw a group on horseback heading our way. There were about ten people in total. Then I noticed a carriage appear, and from it, a young man popped his head out and waved at us.

"Usato!"

"Ah! Kazuki!"

I hadn't heard anything about how we were getting to Luqvist, but now I knew we'd be riding a horse-drawn carriage. Around it were a number of knights in light armor, and one of them was Aruku.

"Blurin, will you be okay?" I asked. "You can't ride in the carriage, you know?"

The grizzly slapped my legs. He growled a message that was all too easy to read:

Of course I won't be okay!

"You get more selfish every day, don't you?" I said.

"You've gotten too strong to understand ordinary people and animals," said Amako.

The grizzly roared in agreement. It ticked me off, so I gave Blurin a good flick in the nose and walked over toward the incoming carriage. I heard the bear growl with fierce intimidation and Amako rush to catch up, but I ignored them both.

"Good morning, Aruku," I said.

Aruku leaped from his horse and put a fist to his chest in greeting.

"Morning!" he said.

The guy was nothing if not energetic.

"I'll load your baggage on the carriage," he said, holding out his arms, "so you two, please board the carriage."

"Oh, thanks. And Blurin?"

"My apologies, but he'll join us outside."

Just as I expected.

I passed my backpack to Aruku. Before Amako and I got in the carriage, I also made sure to remove the baggage from Blurin's back because the grizzly was glaring at me.

"No being a nuisance to Aruku and the knights, okay?"

Blurin growled.

"Don't give me that '*I can't promise anything*' growl, Blurin."

They should be okay. Probably. If it comes down to it, I'll just walk instead of riding in the carriage.

I passed the baggage Blurin was carrying to a knight and hopped inside the carriage. It was easily spacious enough for ten people. I took a brief look around, then looked further into the carriage, where Kazuki and Inukami-senpai were sitting, along with a robed girl with unique blue hair. It was Welcie.

"Morning, everyone," I said.

"It's been quite some time, hasn't it, Usato-sama?" said Welcie.

"You're joining us on this journey, Welcie?"

The girl had left a big impression on me. First there was the way her face flushed when we'd been checking my magical affinity, then the way she freaked out at the sight of Rose.

"Indeed I am," she replied. "I'll be with you as far as Luqvist. I wouldn't want to leave everything entirely on your shoulders, so I'd like to help out where I can."

"I see. Thank you."

I didn't think we'd be left entirely to our own devices, but it was certainly generous of the king to send the kingdom's own mage to support us.

"I feel more confident with you along, Welcie," said senpai.

"Oh, I'm not *that* powerful."

"But you're our magic teacher," said Kazuki. "You should be more confident in yourself."

It was clear that Kazuki and Inukami-senpai really trusted Welcie. As their magic teacher, she was to them what Rose was to me.

Sure would be nice if Welcie could share a little of her gentle aura with Rose. She's like a gentle little animal where Rose is like a ferocious carnivore with a terrifying aura that scares anyone she looks at.

I was just thinking about how saying as much to Rose would only land me a beating when Amako began pulling at my sleeve. She was looking at Welcie with some worry on her face.

"You don't need to worry about her," I said, knowing what was on her mind. "You only need to be careful of senpai."

"Okay, got it."

Inukami-senpai didn't look impressed.

"What? Why do I feel like that was a subtle way of telling her I'm dangerous?" Inukami-senpai said.

I ignored the look on her face and leaned back against the carriage wall. With a clunk, the carriage was off.

"We're on our way," said Kazuki.

"That we are. Welcie, what about the letters?" I asked.

"They're safely with me," Welcie said, taking several letters from a small rucksack. "Suzune-sama and Kazuki-sama already know, but these are the letters to be handed out to each nation. I'll keep ahold of them for now and give you the ones you're responsible for when we part ways at Luqvist."

"When we part ways? But what about the letter for Luqvist?" I asked.

"I will pass out that letter myself. You'll all be with me, of course."

Oh, so does that mean she'll give us an example of how to deliver the letters to people of power? That's a relief. I'm sure it's not just a matter of meeting a national leader, passing them a letter, then leaving.

Kazuki, senpai, and I were all a bit worried because we weren't used to this kind of thing. I leaned back once more against the carriage wall and stared out the window. It was all just green trees. I was used to seeing them, but in just a few hours, I'd be met with sights I'd never seen before.

Our journey had begun, and we were off to new places—a grand adventure filled with danger and the unknown. Like it or not, I was a part of this world now, and I thought vaguely of the days ahead as the carriage continued to rock.

* * *

The Black Knight. Assigned to the second army in the Demon Lord's forces.

It was a name that drew fear and envy from most demons and a name that had come from the sheer strength of the knight's impenetrable armor, a creation of dark magic.

Excellent defensive magic was common among dark magic types, and yet the Black Knight was unique—also equipped with devastating offensive abilities. Her armor was capable of freely changing shape to attack in a variety of different ways, and any attack from the enemy was reflected straight back.

Unique, unrivaled, and wielding the most powerful of magics.

That was the Black Knight.

"Oi! None of this slacking, ya dumb half-wit! Ya want another smack or what?"

I groaned.

What would the other demons think if they saw me like this? If they gazed upon my humiliation?

I'd fallen during my run, utterly exhausted, and now Rose stood over me, her foot twisting into my back. I felt the healing magic seep into my muscles and mend my weary body, but spiritually and mentally, this woman had worn me down—and was still wearing me down.

"Here I was thinkin' you'd come around. Never would've expected you to use that as a getaway opportunity. Do you get any more selfish? Should I take you into the forest again?" she said.

"N-No! Not that!"

The hellscape of those days flashed across my mind. I remembered being chased around by grizzlies even bigger than the one Usato called Blurin, and when I finally got away, I'd faint with exhaustion only to wake from a fearsome hunger.

I watched as a little ball of black fur jumped to Rose's shoulder with a squeak. It came from the stables. The animal looked down at me with its head tilted adorably to the side. It was the same noir rabbit that had betrayed me. I thought it was my friend, but everything went according to *her* plan.

"You realize the gate guards would have caught you in your current state, right?" asked Rose.

I grunted. Usato left today on some kind of journey to deliver letters. It was supposed to be a long trip, and I'd heard he wouldn't be back for at least two or three days. When I heard that, I decided that I would follow him. I didn't think about it; I just did it. However dangerous it was, I figured it would still be better than being here with the Rescue Team.

But it wasn't that easy, and Rose had caught me in no time. Hence the reason I was currently enduring punishment.

"Aren't you . . . worried?" I grunted.

"Worried?" Rose asked. "About what?"

"About Usato!"

She gave me this look, like, *What the hell are you on about?* It rubbed me the wrong way. But however rebellious I might have felt, I was still trapped under this woman's boot, so I kept my mouth shut.

"Not even in the slightest," said Rose. "He's a healer with knowledge that rivals my own. He won't go down without one heck of a fight."

Is she saying that he's slowly turning into another version of herself? Then again, when I think about it, he **is** *like her in some ways. Terrifying smiles, the way they run their hands through their hair . . .*

I'd heard that students ended up like their teachers, but this was nothing to smile about.

"Besides, there's a limit to the training Usato can get here," said Rose. "What he needs now is to experience the rest of the world."

I said nothing in reply. Rose flashed a wicked grin at me.

"Wait a second . . . Are you worried about him?" she asked.

"N-No! It's just all getting on my nerves," I spat back.

I couldn't tell her I wanted to run away from her. I'd only be asking for more punishment if I told her *that.*

"Not that I care," said Rose. "But how long are you going to just lie there? Get up and get back to it!"

I realized then that she'd taken her boot off my back and that my exhaustion was gone.

"F-Fine!"

I jumped to my feet and got back to running laps of the training grounds, a panicked look on my face. As I panted for breath, I thought about how I'd never done much training in the Demon Lord's army. I was so strong it wasn't even necessary. It didn't seem like there was even a point to strengthening my body.

The Demon Lord's army and the Rescue Team. At each of those two places, I was in a completely different position. Until just a little while ago, when I was back in the army, I'd done whatever I felt like, whenever I felt like it, because nobody could stop me.

I was born with a unique magical affinity for dark magic, which quickly made me a subject of fear and awe. What made my dark magic unique was that it worked regardless of whether or not I specifically cast it. As a child, I wrapped myself in black magic often, bringing danger to those around me.

Perhaps that was why, by the time I was aware of the ways of the world, I had been thrown—almost as if abandoned—into the Demon Lord army's training grounds. In the end, I was simply far too much for my parents to handle. They didn't know what to do with me, didn't know how to love me, didn't know what dangers would befall them on account of my unusual dark magic. And so they let me go.

Once that happened, I stayed locked within my armor. Or more accurately, by that time, the inside of that armor was the only place I felt at ease. Nobody could hurt me. Nobody could even touch me.

I shunned the world around me. I fought and I felled my enemies for little more than my own satisfaction, and the days passed by. As far as I was concerned, the Demon Lord's army was nothing more than a way for me to kill time.

"But . . ." I muttered.

But now I don't have my armor.

And yet I didn't feel ill at ease the way I once had. I still did not understand why. Where I was now, the Rescue Team? Even if you threatened me with death, I'd never say it was better than the Demon Lord's army.

But something in me was, perhaps, changing. I felt myself wondering about this as I ran, and then something collided with the back of my head.

"Ouch?!" I cried.

I rubbed the back of my head and turned around.

"What are you spacin' out for!" shouted Rose, looking like she'd just swung something with her right arm. "Run!"

What did she just do?!

Probably, she'd thrown something at me. What, I didn't know. I covered my head and picked up my pace.

"This is all *his* fault," I muttered.

The constant abuse from Rose, the weird feeling of fulfillment each day, all of it was because of Usato, who'd left today.

"I'll get you, Usato!"

And the next time we met, I'd make sure he got it.

* * *

Luqvist was a neighbor of the Llinger Kingdom.

There was a gigantic building there, easily mistaken for a castle, that was in fact a school for studying magic. It was there that we would find the most powerful person in Luqvist, a person who, back in my world, would be called a principal or headmaster.

The children who attended Luqvist's school started their study with general magic, then studied each affinity, sometimes competing and sometimes fighting, but always polishing their skills.

According to Aruku, one could also learn swordsmanship and combat skills in Luqvist. Welcie said that those who graduated with the best records were, generally speaking, powerful spellcasters. Amako added that there was often discrimination based on the type of magic a person was born with.

When two mages of the same magic affinity wanted to determine who was better, they could do so based on magic power, their magical senses, or their skill level, all of which could be improved through effort. The magic you were born with, however, could never be changed no matter how hard you worked.

* * *

It was the night of our sixth day since leaving Llinger Kingdom. I was thinking about Luqvist as I sat in front of our campfire. Everyone except for the knights on guard duty was asleep. I knew that I should have been doing the same, but I just couldn't seem to fall asleep, knowing that we'd reach Luqvist tomorrow.

"Don't feel like you have to stay up on my account, okay?" I said to Aruku, who sat across from me.

Aruku smiled.

"Don't worry about me. I got a lot of rest earlier."

I'd left the carriage feeling restless and unable to sleep, and when Aruku noticed, he was kind enough to sit up and talk with me.

"You stayed in Luqvist for a time, right?" I asked.

"I did . . ." said Aruku, a slight frown on his face.

"I'm sorry. Is it better if I don't ask about it?"

"No, not at all," Aruku said, playing it down with a wave of his hand before putting his sword on the ground beside him. "It's fine. And though you're going to learn for yourself soon enough, I can tell you a few things myself."

"Like what?"

"You heard from Amako that Luqvist discriminates based on magical affinity, right?"

"Yeah . . ."

I'd heard about it from Welcie and Amako on our way here. It sounded awful, but I also felt somewhat distant and disconnected from it. Kazuki and Inukami-senpai were enraged, but I still wasn't sure exactly what to think about it.

"The magical affinity discrimination is bad enough on its own, but there's another thing you should know about too: demi-human discrimination."

"They have that too?"

It wasn't just Luqvist—other nations discriminated against demi-humans too. At least, that was what I'd heard.

"The people who visit Luqvist all have their own reasons for devoting themselves to their studies," Aruku continued. "Maybe they want to become knights, or perhaps they have their sights set on wealth . . . It would take too long to cover every potential motivation, but what matters is that some of those people, the demi-humans, go to Luqvist knowing they will face persecution."

"You mean they understand that they're putting themselves in danger?"

"Yes. That's how much value Luqvist has."

It made me think of the elite school systems back in my own world with their power hierarchies. But I couldn't believe a place would be so important that people would be willing to put themselves in harm's way. Why was magic training so important? It sounded like hell.

You get the pulp beaten out of you. Then you get thrown all over the place, and when you wake up, it happens again. And when you think you've gotten out of the way of one attack, you get kicked instead. I couldn't believe anyone would willingly put themselves through that kind of purely physical training.

It was like demi-humans were going to school just to get beaten up.

"You look like you're having trouble wrapping your head around it," said Aruku.

"I guess I am. I don't get it."

"Think of it this way: those students have a goal that they must see completed, even if it means putting themselves in danger. On an official level, Luqvist forbids the trafficking and oppression of demi-humans, but its students come from all across the world. Though some have no interest in discrimination, others carry a hatred that goes beyond reason."

Aruku shot me a pained smile and threw some wood upon the fire. As it burned more brightly, I felt as if I saw a certain sadness in his expression.

"There is no better place for learning magic than Luqvist," said Aruku. "But for a small percentage of people, the place is hell. To be honest, I don't like it much."

"I'm sorry."

"Oh, no! You did nothing wrong, Sir Usato! I came because I want to be of service, and I thought about this all very thoroughly before taking this responsibility!"

Still, in the end, it was me who had asked him to join me to this place that some people thought of as hell. I felt awful for doing it.

"Er . . . Uh . . . Oh! How do you see the demi-human people, Sir Usato?" asked Aruku.

"See them? Hm . . ."

To say they were different from humans felt too vague, but so far, I'd only met and talked to Amako, who was a beastkin, and Felm, who was a demon.

When I look at them, what do I see?

"I don't see them as all that different," I said.

I didn't know if it was because of a bad influence of some kind or if it was because I had a captain who was more of a monster than any demi-human I could imagine, but I didn't think of demi-humans as all that frightening.

When I told Aruku as much, his eyes grew a little wide, but in the next instant, he burst into the kind of laughter that was completely out of character for him.

Did I say something weird? Why is he laughing like that?

"Not all that different, you say . . . I should have expected that from you."

"Is that something I would say?"

"Very much so. It's why Amako feels safe with you. Because you treat demi-humans as you treat humans."

So basically, my view on demi-humans is so different from the humans here that what I said was laughable? I guess the people of my world must see things pretty differently from the people of this one.

For me, everything I saw was different, and I suppose from magic to demi-humans, I lumped them all together and saw them the same way. But for people born here, magic was a part of the everyday, and demi-humans were scary.

"You can say you expected that from me, but I don't think I'm that good of a person," I said.

"Ah, but you are, Sir Usato. You just don't know it yourself."

"Let's not go putting me on a pedestal, yeah?"

I noticed the frown and the sadness seemed to have left Aruku's face, replaced by a kindly smile. He'd been a bit stiff and insistent on proper manners at the start, but now I could tell he was opening up.

I was listening to the sounds of the campfire and staring into the darkness of the surrounding plains when Aruku tilted his head curiously. He was looking behind me, over my right shoulder.

"What's up?" I asked.

"Seems like you're not the only one who can't sleep."

He was looking in the direction of the carriage. Curious, I did so myself. The carriage door was open, even though I remembered closing it when I left. From the shadows, a face emerged. It belonged to a young beastkin girl. Amako.

Her ears moved as she looked at us dejectedly. Then, when she met my eyes, she walked over.

"Can't sleep?" I asked.

"Let's put it this way," she said, sitting by my side and staring at the campfire flames. "*Someone* won't let me sleep."

I could see the smooth luster of her hair shining in the dim light of the fire.

But why this late at night? I thought Amako was supposed to be sleeping soundly by senpai's side. Wait a second. What does she mean that someone *won't let her sleep?*

"I woke up when Suzune wrapped me in her arms."

Aruku laughed.

"Sounds like it isn't easy for you, Amako."

"Not in the slightest."

"She just can't help herself," I muttered with a sigh.

I knew that Inukami-senpai didn't have any bad intentions, so I couldn't help but smile at the stone-faced Amako.

"What are you talking about?" asked Amako.

"Tomorrow, and Luqvist."

I got her up to speed, though I skipped the parts about demi-human discrimination. It was just a barebones rundown.

"I have friends in Luqvist," said Amako.

"Oh? Beastkin?"

"Yes. They let me stay with them while I was there, when I didn't know where to go."

I wondered if they were like the demi-humans Aruku had mentioned, who went to Luqvist to study.

"Do you want to see them again?" I asked.

"Yes."

Of course you do.

"I don't know if they're still there," said Amako. "But once things are wrapped up in Luqvist, then . . ."

Amako trailed off and looked down at the floor. It was clear she wanted to see them as soon as possible but didn't feel like she could say as much.

"Then you should go and see them," I said. "You don't have to worry about us."

I wouldn't be able to take her while we were delivering our letter.

Amako looked up at me for a moment before speaking.

"I want you to come," she said.

"Huh? Me? Won't I just get in the way?"

Amako shook her head.

"No. And I want to introduce them to the person who's helping me."

Demi-humans living in Luqvist. What do I do if they're really scary?

I didn't think I'd meet anyone as scary as Rose, but I was still really worried about whom I'd be meeting. Luqvist wasn't a safe place for demi-humans to live, so there was every chance that Amako's friends were rough individuals.

In any case, I figured I'd check with Aruku for permission.

"Aruku, do you think it would be okay for me to accompany Amako to see her friends after we deliver our letter?"

"I think so. We'll have to stay in Luqvist while a decision is made regarding the king's letter, so we'll be able to make time."

"Shouldn't be a problem then," I said.

I glanced at Amako, who held her own legs to her chest happily, likely glad at the knowledge she'd be able to meet up with old friends. When I thought about it, I realized that she'd spent a long time living away from her own people.

When I was her age, I was little more than a cheeky coward.

I couldn't help but chuckle at the comparison.

"Think I might finally get some shut-eye," I said.

I felt better after talking to Aruku and Amako, and I'd gotten sleepy. I'd resigned myself to pulling an all-nighter, but now I felt like I'd be able to get some sleep. I was just about to stand up when Aruku stopped me.

"Sir Usato," he said, looking to my side. "You might want to reconsider."

"Reconsider?"

I hadn't noticed because I'd been so lost in my own thoughts, but Amako was asleep, balled up as she held her own knees, breathing softly. Perhaps it was because she finally felt safe and at ease. In any case, at some point she'd grabbed ahold of the hem of my shirt, and Aruku had stopped me from standing so as not to wake her.

"She really does feel safest at your side," he said.

"I guess I'm sleeping under the stars tonight," I replied. "What about you, Aruku?"

"It's not much longer until I'm due for guard duty, but . . . are you going to sleep sitting up?"

"It's no problem," I said. "I'm used to it now."

When I'd been left to fend for myself in the forest, I couldn't lie down and sleep because I had to be ready to run suddenly if monsters appeared. I'd gotten completely accustomed to sleeping this way. I laid Amako on her side, then took my Rescue Team coat and put it over her like a blanket.

"Well then, see you tomorrow, Aruku."

"Good night."

I closed my eyes and thought vaguely of how it had been a while since I'd last slept outside. And perhaps I was more tired than I thought, because I quickly drifted off to sleep.

* * *

". . . -kun . . ."

Someone was calling my name. I opened my eyes from a light slumber.

When did I end up lying down?

The last thing I remembered was sitting in front of the fire with Amako and falling asleep just like that. Now my head was resting on something soft, like a pillow.

"Wakey wakey, Usato-kun."

"Hm?"

I was still braindead from having just woken up. I looked up at the face peering down at me. But even with my brain still trying to wake up, I knew the face immediately.

"Oh. It's you," I said.

"Wh-What?! I think a more surprised and bashful reaction is in order when you wake up on a girl's legs!"

Inukami-senpai made her thoughts and intentions as clear as day. I got up from her legs and looked around. The sun was up and it was bright outside. I must have overslept. We were inside the carriage, and aside from Amako, everyone else was awake.

"Did you carry me in here, Kazuki?" I asked.

"Hm? Oh, yeah, but don't sweat it. You're pretty heavy, but it wasn't any trouble."

I guess it's different when you rest around people you trust.

In the Rescue Team, oversleeping wasn't tolerated. It was an implicit rule. So it felt like it had been a long time since I'd been able to sleep and wake the way I had today.

"But do something about senpai, would you?" said Kazuki with a wry grin.

"Huh? You mean Inukami-senpai?"

I turned from Kazuki to look at her. She was sulking and muttering under her breath as she patted Amako's head as she was still sleeping.

But, uh . . . exactly what is she doing?

"How rude," she said. "You didn't even get a little bit excited at waking up on a beautiful young girl's legs."

"That's because you make yourself so obvious. And about referring to yourself as a beautiful young lady . . ."

Though truth be told, she *was* very beautiful.

And if I were being totally honest, I was happy to wake up with my head on her legs. But I also wasn't the kind of fish to just go happily biting on fishing hooks either.

"Come on," I sighed. "No need to get all sulky. It's not like I wasn't excited about it . . . probably."

Perhaps my words hit the mark, because Inukami-senpai cleared her throat and removed her hand from Amako's head.

"Usato-kun, I don't know why you're not more honest with yourself."

Kazuki laughed.

"Yeah, you're surprisingly warped," he said in agreement.

I wasn't about to let this go without saying something.

"No, no. You two sit too far on the honest side of the spectrum," I said. "Me? This? I'm normal."

"No, you're not," said Kazuki and Inukami-senpai in chorus.

I guess as far as they were concerned, my reaction to things wasn't normal.

"I would say you're a little . . . different from normal, Usato-sama," said Welcie, who looked up from her papers for a moment to add her piece and chuckle.

"Not you too!" I groaned.

And if Amako was awake, I bet she'd jump on the "Usato isn't normal" bandwagon too.

I slumped back against the wall of the carriage. Now *I* was the one doing the sulking. I didn't have anything better to do, so I started doing the practice that Rose told me to keep up. I tried intensifying my healing magic. When Welcie saw it, she let out a surprised gasp.

"You see? You're *not* normal," she said.

"What? No, this isn't all that difficult, really," I said.

Whenever I did this inside the carriage, she said something about it. When I asked about it, Welcie said that people couldn't usually handle the practice I was doing when they had as little experience as me. I tried to tell Welcie that anyone could do it so long as they knew *how* to do it.

"That's what I've been telling you," Welcie said. "It may be easy, but it's also very dangerous. If you make any sort of mistake, then you lose control and you might lose a hand in the explosion. You might think it's all fine because you're a healer, but . . . that sort of training should be done only after you have better control of your magic."

And so she went on lecturing me about it while I kept on practicing. I deepened the color of my healing magic until it was a little lighter than Orga's, and then I returned it to its usual color. And then I did it again. According to Welcie, I had developed a pretty good grasp on it, but I couldn't really tell just by looking, so I didn't feel like I understood it that well.

"I wonder if I can do that?" muttered Inukami-senpai.

"You have a kind of reckless side to you, so I don't think it's a good idea," I said.

"As long as *you're* here, there's no problem though, no?" she said.

No, no. We're talking like it's easy, but I'm doing my utmost here. If you picked this up like it was nothing, I think I might die of shame.

At the same time, I also simply didn't want senpai doing anything so extremely dangerous. Thanks to my training, I had pretty good pain tolerance, but that one time my hand burst really hurt. I wasn't certain that a girl like senpai would be able to stand that kind of pain.

"Stop that! Stop that, Suzune-sama! You can't do such a thing unless you have Usato-sama's level of control—" Welcie exclaimed.

"Oh come on, Welcie. You're curious too, aren't you, Kazuki?"

"Hm . . . I won't say I'm not," replied Kazuki, "but if Usato thinks we shouldn't, then I think he's probably right."

"Hmph. Well, I don't want to cause him too much trouble."

Which you are already doing, I thought but did not say.

I let out a sigh when Inukami-senpai finally gave up, then asked Welcie something I'd been thinking about.

"How much further until we reach Luqvist?"

"Based on how we're going, we should make it there by noon, when the sun reaches its peak."

Which means perhaps one or two hours. This place doesn't have clocks, so it's all a bit of a guess.

A city of students. There was a lot of intrigue surrounding the place. There was the discrimination against demi-humans and magical affinities, and there were Amako's friends, but there was one thing I was more curious about than anything else: the Luqvist healer.

* * *

"Commander of the third army, Amila Vergrett," said the Demon Lord. "Regarding your failure in the last battle . . ."

My error had been costly. So costly we had lost the battle that would have led to the invasion of Llinger Kingdom.

"Sir!" I said.

Our forces were easily strong enough to overcome the Llinger Kingdom's army, but all the same, the army I led had lost, and we were forced into ignominious retreat. The casualty count was high, and we had also lost Baljinak, one of our aces. My position as commander was as good as gone.

"I am painfully aware of the extent to which I have failed you," I said, "and I am prepared to end my own life at your order. I will make no excuses."

"No, you are far too valuable and powerful in my army for that. I will not lose you for a lone error. However, I am surprised that the humans put up such a fight."

The demon lord lazed in his throne and let a smile slip across his face.

"Sir?"

"Hmph. I do not smile for our loss. But it is very interesting what the humans have shown us: that they intend to fight."

"But . . . what do you mean?" I asked.

We had been attempting to invade their land—it was only natural that the humans would defend themselves.

"The humans I know are not worthy playthings. They obey when they are intimidated. They give in to their desires when tempted. They jump as high as you ask at the sight of money. There is nothing as stupid as a human. There is no creature so stupid that has propagated to such an extent. Do you not think so, Amila?" the Demon Lord mused.

I remained silent.

"This is why I did my work as the Demon Lord: to rid the world of humans. I befuddled them with my cunning, incited them to kill one another, and stained the lands with their blood."

The Demon Lord spoke the words as if they were nothing. Looking upon the joy on his face filled me with relief at the fact that he was not my enemy.

"However, I suffered defeat at the hands of these humans," said the Demon Lord. "Thoroughly and completely. But it was not their combined might that did it—rather, it was an overwhelmingly strong individual among them, fighting on their own."

"Overwhelmingly strong?"

"That they were. Even hundreds of years later, I remember it as though it were yesterday."

The Demon Lord narrowed his eyes as if reliving the memories. For him, the battle against the foe who had sealed his powers would not simply disappear with time. And yet somehow, that foe really had felled the Demon Lord, who here before me radiated the aura of an indomitable force. I could not even begin to imagine such a person.

"Just one person, for no particular cause or reason, destroyed my army, cut me down, and became a hero. It is a name that disgusts you, is it not?"

"It is . . ."

Many soldiers had been lost at the hands of the heroes. When we had been forced into retreat, I lost count of the number of times I wished I had entered the fray earlier.

"I understand how you must feel," said the Demon Lord. "It vexes you, doesn't it? You think of how different it would have been had they not been there. Anybody would think the same."

He paused for a moment to look down on me with a wicked grin.

"But the humans are stupid. They detest that which defies the world as they understand it, and they attempt to destroy it. Even if it is their own kind."

"The humans attacked their own hero?"

"I created the spark. I gave them the push they needed, and they responded marvelously. A few days later, I crushed them."

It was just like the Demon Lord to do so.

"Might I be so bold as to offer an opinion?" I asked.

"Speak."

"The country that summoned the heroes is the Llinger Kingdom. Perhaps there was little meaning in use of the strategy you speak of. That is, having the humans betray one another."

"I never intended to use it. That kingdom has not changed in the slightest. And besides, it was I who ordered the invasion."

"My apologies!"

How foolish of me to speak an opinion without understanding the Demon Lord's intent. Perhaps there truly is nothing left but for me to end my own life. Is there any reason for me to continue to serve? My master, I apologize for being so useless a disciple.

"You look ready for death," said the Demon Lord. "You must be punished."

"My life, then? I understand. Consider it done."

"You may do so if you wish, but . . . do you lean towards self-harm?"

He watched me with some curiosity, tears in my eyes as my sword wavered in my hands. But just as quickly, he seemed to lose interest entirely.

"You are demoted," he said. "As of today, you are no longer a commander."

"Sir . . ."

If not death, then a demotion was only natural. I was too inexperienced for a position of such leadership. I felt gloom fill my features, but the Demon Lord grinned.

"You are earnest," he said, standing from his throne and walking toward me as I bowed before him. I lowered my head, shocked, as his feet stopped right in front of me.

"Amila, you are not suited to the position of commander," he said slowly. "You are meant to fight. To run rampant on the battlefield, and to see your enemy standing before you."

His words came as a shock. I remained silent as he went on.

"Titles and ranks have no meaning. In this world, all that matters is whether you are strong or weak. The powerless die. Amila, do you wish to be strong?"

"Yes, sir!"

"Then you are not meant to be a commander. You are not meant to waste your days leading troops. This battle has taught us such. As a soldier, you will be put to far better use."

Each and every one of those words changed everything for me. I had been proud of my position as commander. I trained troops and I led them. It was my honor to stand above them and carry out my duties. But now I understood my true purpose.

"As of today," I said, "I will no longer be commander. As a soldier, I will use all the skills I have honed and everything I have, in service to you, my lord!"

"You speak the truth?"

"Yes, sir!"

The Demon Lord nodded and returned to his throne.

Why did I fight? Until now, it had been to kill Rose, who had hurt my teacher, and to kill the heroes, who had ended so many of my comrades.

But now, I finally understood.

I needed no grudge or hate to fuel my sword. I needed only my loyalty to the Demon Lord. And with that, I could let go of my position as commander and become a soldier—a sword to annihilate his enemies.

CHAPTER 7

Welcome to Luqvist, the School of Magic!

It had been one week since we left Llinger Kingdom. Thanks to Amako's prescience, we'd managed to avoid any major trouble and arrive at Luqvist without issue. We'd still been attacked by monsters along the way, but according to Welcie, the encounter rate was totally different than usual.

Blurin also acted as a good monster deterrent because he was an especially strong monster type himself, but even then, Amako's power was super convenient.

The gates of Luqvist loomed before us, and I poked my head from the carriage window to take in their size.

"So pretty . . ." I awed.

The gates of Llinger gave off old, sturdy vibes, but these were grandiose—largely black with some flashes of other colors decorating them. There was something that looked like a magical seal inscribed on them, which told us that maybe they weren't just ordinary gates.

"Kind of feels like a school," I said.

"But nothing like any school we've been to," said Kazuki, also poking his head out the window.

Welcie hopped out of the carriage and, together with a few knights, approached the guards at the gate to talk about letting us through. I knew we had to be careful when we got inside.

We were representatives of the Llinger Kingdom now, so we couldn't do anything to sully its reputation.

"Senpai, please be on your best behavior," I said. "No getting into any fights, okay?"

"Let's not forget I was head of the student council," she said. "I'm a rule follower. I won't cause any trouble. Why don't you trust me more?"

"Because you were the head of the student council," I said.

Inukami-senpai had a strong sense of justice. If she saw a student being bullied, there was a good chance she'd dive right in to help them.

An impressive set of principles, that.

"And don't forget to wear that cloak I gave you, okay, Amako?" I said. "Do your best to keep that tail under control."

"I'll be fine. I've done this before."

Amako put her cloak on. It was the same color as my Rescue Team one. She wouldn't be going with us to the castle though. Amako was going to stay with Aruku and the carriage. It was much safer for her with him than it was with us, given the responsibilities we had to see through.

As for who was going to the castle, it was Welcie, Kazuki, senpai, and myself.

"We've got permission," said Welcie, her voice ringing from outside the carriage. "Let's head inside."

The carriage began to move again. The huge gates opened, and the city revealed itself. A variety of big buildings stood next to one another, all of them white and exuding cleanliness.

The city was very similar to Llinger Kingdom. The main street was its center, with buildings on either side and streets between the buildings. Just like in Llinger, the streets were lined with stalls, but unlike in the kingdom, the people running them were all kids about the same age as me, dressed in uniform-like robes. Everyone walking the streets wore the same robes. It was a truly strange sight—I could count the number of adults I saw on a single hand.

"So this is the City of Magic . . ." I said.

I hadn't expected the kids here to have so much freedom. I'd imagined it more like the schools I went to in my home world, where everything was built on set rules. What I was seeing was less like a high school and much more like a university.

"We'll have trouble navigating the roads by carriage from here, so we'll walk the rest of the way," said Welcie.

"Oh, okay," I said, and then, "What about Blurin?"

"Your blue grizzly will be taken to the stables with the horses. He'll draw too much attention in town."

That made sense. I was glad to know we wouldn't have to worry about scaring anyone as we took him through the city streets.

We all got out of the carriage.

"What *is* this?" I asked.

I didn't like the weight of the gazes on us. We were still barely through the main gates, and already kids were gathering to stare at us like we were some rare creatures. All of them wore black robes, which made me feel even more out of place in my white uniform.

I noticed a boy, different from the others. His robe was dirty with soot.

"Usato? What's wrong?" Kazuki asked me.

He looked pale, and there was something about his gloomy eyes that differed from those around him.

"Nothing," I said, "it's just . . ."

When our eyes met and he realized I was looking at him, he trembled and took off somewhere.

"Kazuki?" I asked. "Do I have a menacing gaze? Do I look scary?"

Kazuki looked surprised by my question.

"Not menacing, but courageous," he said.

I felt like I was a long, long way from that, but hearing it from Kazuki made me happy all the same.

"Courageous . . . People always called me timid, so that . . . means a lot to me."

I trembled at the thought of it, and then Welcie pointed down the main street, at the biggest and most noticeable building in the whole city.

"It's not very far now," she said. "The knights can stay here while we head off to deliver the letter. Kazuki-sama, Suzune-sama, Usato-sama, please follow me."

"Take care of Blurin please, Amako," I said.

"Okay. We'll be waiting for you," replied Amako with a nod.

I hoped that we'd be back soon. I promised her that we'd go to see her friends. We said our temporary goodbyes to the knights and walked along the main street with Welcie taking the lead.

"My weapons are sturdy and cheap! I've got a world of confidence in them! Buy here, buy now, at Karlguna Weapons!" someone shouted.

"Nobody beats our jerky! Don't go underestimating me just because I'm a student!" another person shouted.

"I'll buy anything! Also, happy to talk trade, so don't be shy!" yet another person called out.

Wow, there really are *a whole lot of different shops here.*

It couldn't have been easy for kids to manage their stalls, but I was in awe—some of them were even younger than me.

"Many of the kids who aren't particularly wealthy spend their time outside of classes working," said Welcie. "Many of the stores are actually managed by adults, but the ones working them are more often than not students."

"Kind of like a part-time job, then."

Interesting. It's just like back home—people working on the side while they study.

I walked through the streets pretty quickly to make sure I didn't lose sight of Welcie, but despite that, I was still able to take in the Luqvist scenery. It pained me to think that a place as lively as this suffered from discrimination issues. When I saw people passing by—kids, really, the same age as me—and smiling as they looked at the different stalls, I honestly started wondering if there really *was* discrimination in Luqvist.

I wonder what Kazuki and senpai think about the place so far? Maybe I'll just ask them.

"What do you think so far, senpai?" I asked. "This place must be so fascinating for you . . . huh?"

Inukami-senpai was gone. I looked around but I couldn't see her anywhere.

"Kazuki, Welcie, where's senpai?" I asked.

"Senpai? Uh . . . where'd she . . . ?" Kazuki stuttered.

"Suzune-sama is right . . . She's gone!" Welcie exclaimed.

"That girl . . . can't she stay settled for even just a few minutes?!"

We hadn't even been here ten minutes and already she'd disappeared. I looked around with a frown, and then I heard something.

"This is *such* a wizardry city! Everything for sale is straight out of a fantasy novel!"

The voice came from behind me, and it was one I knew all too well. I couldn't see exactly where it was coming from, but I had a rough idea. I turned away from Kazuki and Welcie without a word and headed for Inukami-senpai. She was sure to be drawing attention to herself. After all, she was way too excited, and she was a beautiful young woman on top of it. Unfortunately, she was crushing the image of her that I kept inside of me.

"Sorry!" I said as I weaved through the crowd of onlookers. "She's with me! I kind of wish she wasn't, but she is!"

Inukami-senpai was fully dressed in Llinger Kingdom's own custom-made equipment. Of course she was going to stand out among a crowd of black robes. I pushed through the seemingly endless crowd, sighing like I had never sighed before.

She is having way, way too much fun here. It's cringeworthy to think of how little hope she had in our old world.

"Just . . . a little . . . further . . ." I grunted.

I'd finally gotten to a point that I could see her up ahead. Her eyes were alight as she looked at some equipment, so excited she was practically drooling. She was like a kid in a candy store. I picked up my pace but accidentally bumped my shoulder into someone who got in the way.

"Ah! Sorry!" I cried.

The person fell to their butt with a gasp of surprise. I felt bad for them, so I tentatively reached out a hand, but . . . I let out my own gasp of surprise when I saw the almond-shaped eyes that looked up at me.

They were like Amako's—they were beastkin eyes. Her head was covered by the hood of her robe so I could only make out a face. If they were hiding themselves on a day as sunny as this one, it was likely because of their race. I'd never imagined I'd encounter a beastkin so soon, but I also had to think of the situation. I pretended not to notice.

"Are you okay?" I asked.

The robed figure's eyes grew wide. She took my hand, looked at me from head to toe, then slowly stood to her feet.

"You're not from around here," she said, brushing the dust off her robe. "It's rare to see visitors at this time."

The voice was female. I laughed.

"Is it really that rare?" I asked.

The girl glanced at me, then waved her hand to show me she didn't need me to worry.

"Just a fall," she said. "I'm not hurt."

"That's good to hear. I'd love to stay and properly apologize but I'm kind of in a hurry," I said.

I have to go grab that overexcited child and take her back to Kazuki and Welcie.

"I'm sorry for bumping into you," I said as I took a step toward Inukami-senpai.

"Wait."

"Wha?!"

I felt something clutch my right arm and I was suddenly pulled backward. I turned and met the eyes of the girl, her head still completely covered by her hood, her gaze piercing straight into me. Then she brought my arm to her face and sniffed it. I didn't have a chance to think about how weird that was because I felt such rage and murder from her.

"I know this scent . . ." she said.

"What are you talking about?"

She doesn't mean I have body odor, does she? If it's not that, then . . .

"Don't play dumb with me," she said. "Why do you have my friend's scent on you?"

"Oh, I don't suppose you're the person who took care of a girl by the name of Amako, are—"

Before I could finish, the girl's hand gripped my arm hard, like a vise. She was strong. Not as strong as Rose, but powerful all the same. At the very least, I knew it wasn't a human power.

"You're coming with me," she said.

The girl tried to pull me away from the crowd, but I couldn't leave yet, so I dug my heels in and held back. The hooded girl seemed surprised.

"So you refuse. I suppose that must mean Amako is already . . . Hm. And now I'm next, is that it?"

"Wait a second. Let's take a deep breath and calm down. This is all a misunderstanding."

"Calm down?!"

This was getting way out of hand. I felt like she was turning me into some kind of monster.

The girl's left hand, which had grabbed my arm, revealed itself from her robe, and was covered with a gauntlet, and she was squeezing my arm tight. The crowd around me must have noticed it too because they let out gasps of shock and drew away from us.

"What are you? A slave driver? A bandit? Or are you one of the infamous Llinger kidnappers?"

Sorry, but that last one might be my colleagues. They might seem like a rough bunch, but I can assure you it's not that kind of kidnapping.

"Wait! Please, really! Calm down! I'm . . . Amako and me . . . we're friends!"

"Friends? You humans throw that word around so casually . . ."

"Wait!"

But before I could finish, I felt power run through the girl's other arm and all of the surrounding air gathered around her other fist. I couldn't see it, but I heard the unique sound of rushing air from the girl's fist, and I didn't like it. I tried to shake my arm free to run, but it was clamped tight in her vise-like grip, and it was no use.

The girl let out a roar as she punched me in my stomach with one of her steel gauntlets. At the same time, the hood covering her head fell loose, revealing her face in its entirety, along with the ears on her head.

They were rounded beast ears, popping out from her long, brown hair. Her beautiful features were twisted with rage, and though I couldn't grasp what it was she wanted, I resigned myself to catching her fist with my free left hand.

The force of her blow hit directly on my palm.

Just a month ago, I would have passed out from the sheer pain of it. But having gone through the hell of being Rose's punching bag, this wasn't going to be enough to put me down. The moment I thought that, however, something like a blade shot from the gauntlet, cutting my hand open.

"Ouch?!" I cried as blood sprayed from my palm.

I cringed at the slight pain but immediately healed it with my magic. I'd felt myself being cut, but my healing magic was too quick for light cuts to be too much of an issue.

"You took my punch . . . and you healed yourself?! Are you . . . even human?!"

"Of course I'm human!"

How rude! How dare you put me in the same category as Rose!

She couldn't believe that I had just taken her punch and was still standing right there in front of her. Fear flashed across her face as she released my right arm. She had her fists ready to defend herself as she started backing up.

"I'm drawing too much attention," she uttered, suddenly aware of all the eyes on her. She threw her robe back over her head with a scowl.

"I won't forget you," she said ominously as she ran off into a nearby alley.

"Maybe I should go after her?" I pondered.

I knew I could catch her, but I also knew we were here on important business, and I had to keep that in mind.

"Guess I'll just tell Amako about it later, then," I stated.

The girl *did* say she knew Amako, so maybe Amako could just sort out the misunderstanding for us later. If worse came to worst, I guess I'd just have to force the hooded girl to listen to reason.

"But I guess putting myself aside, this is good news for Amako," I continued to myself.

Amako *did* say the beastkin had taken care of her.

Oh, that's right. There's still a crowd gathered around me.

I felt rude gazes hovering over me, like people watching a monster. I wiped the blood from my hand and walked over to Inukami-senpai, who was still fawning over the items at the stall she was at.

She didn't even notice a thing!

I didn't see Kazuki or Welcie around, so I had wished that at least Inukami-senpai would have noticed.

"Inukami-senpai," I said.

"Oh, Usato-kun. Great timing. Look at this. Have you ever seen anything so detailed? So elaborate?"

"Senpai."

"Yeah, I know I already use a sword, but I'm wondering if I should pick up the bow too."

"Inukami!"

"Huh?! F-Fine!" she said, her cheeks flushing red. "I'm going! But don't use my name like that!"

Inukami-senpai put the gear she was holding back where she found it and turned away from me, hurrying to Kazuki and Welcie. I guess she must have felt my frustration in the way I used her name without the usual addition of "senpai." Not that I was all that angry, really.

Fortunately, Welcie and Kazuki hadn't seen any of what happened because of the crowds, so nobody said anything about my scuffle with the beastkin girl. I say "fortunately" because I was worried that I was in the wrong for causing a disturbance with a resident of Luqvist.

"I brought senpai back," I announced.

"Suzune-sama," said Welcie. "Please don't forget that you shoulder a great responsibility."

"Yeah, I'm sorry. I just couldn't contain my excitement."

"Please don't make trouble for us," pleaded Kazuki. "Usato, everything okay?"

"Yep. A bit tiring," I said, smiling, "but otherwise fine."

We walked on.

We'd literally just arrived in Luqvist and I'd already run into trouble.

It made me very anxious.

About ten minutes after we set off again, we arrived at our destination, a huge white building. It seemed bigger the more we looked at it. It looked less like a castle and more like a luxurious school building.

"This is the place, then?" I asked.

"Yes. This is the heart of Luqvist. This is the reason it is known as the City of Wizardry. This is the Luqvist School of Magic."

The Luqvist School of Magic. The first recipient of our letters. Perhaps because the place surpassed what I had imagined it to be, I found myself feeling restless. It was kind of painful being stared at so suspiciously by all the students around us. I could even hear some of them saying things like, "Who're they?" and "That one is kind of plain and boring."

Yep. They're so right I can't even make a counterargument.

"Will they let us inside?" I inquired.

"Yes," said Welcie. "They will have already heard from the guards I spoke to earlier."

"Ah, so someone's coming to welcome us, then?" I asked.

I wonder how they'll treat us? It's not entirely out of the question that they might treat us with some cruelty, but we are *messengers from a neighboring country. Maybe they won't be welcoming exactly, but as long as they treat us okay, I guess . . .*

"Oh, nice outfit."

The sudden voice was like a whisper in my ear, and I screamed in surprise. I leaped back before I could think. It was a kind of creepy I'd never experienced before.

Is it Inukami-senpai trying something again?! No, that voice wasn't hers.

When I looked at the person standing behind me, I found a young boy with gray hair wearing a gentle smile. He laughed.

"I apologize if I frightened you," he said. "I assume you are all part of the envoy from Llinger Kingdom."

"Y-Yes, that is correct," said Welcie. "May I ask your name?"

"My name is Halpha. The headmistress asked me to act as your guide."

His robe fluttered as he dropped into a polite bow.

I initially thought that Halpha was a male, but his face seemed a little androgynous. He was shorter than me, and I couldn't tell what sex he was because of the robes covering his body. To be honest, I wasn't sure.

But more than that, it was even stranger to me that I didn't notice him getting so close he could whisper in my ear. There were lots of people around, sure, but I wasn't the type to let my guard down in a place I was visiting for the first time.

Whoever Halpha was, he wasn't your ordinary guide.

"Usato-kun, is he really a boy or a girl with boyishly good looks?"

"Senpai, I'm about to lose my cool entirely. A little quieter, please!"

"Someone's unusually snappy!"

I really, really needed her to learn how to be a little more low-key sometimes.

We followed Halpha into the school grounds. In the center of the school was a main square, with all the school's buildings built around it. The school square was filled with robed students using their time to do things like read books and practice magic. It was exactly what Inukami-senpai had imagined it would be.

"Whoa . . ." she gasped.

It was so fantastical and lively. I couldn't help staring at everything I saw.

"You seem intrigued by our students," said Halpha, still leading us ahead.

"It's not something we're very used to seeing," replied Inukami-senpai. "I apologize if we're being rude."

"No, no, not rude in the slightest. In fact, we welcome it. For our students, it's an honor to have people such as yourselves take interest in them."

Inukami replied with the flicker of a smile. Kazuki's and Welcie's eyes went wide with surprise. But I wasn't all that shocked. I mean, this was Inukami-senpai and Kazuki we were talking about. They had a presence that most others didn't, like an aura.

"Has the headmistress told you of us?" I asked.

"No," said Halpha, "but I can tell from your dress and your magic power that you're no ordinary guests. That, and . . ."

The young boy spun and poked a finger right at me.

Is there something behind me? But there's nobody behind me. Wait, he's pointing at *me. But he can't be. I don't stand out. All I have going for me is this basic healing magic. Well, that and this uniform that marks me as a member of the Rescue Team.*

"You are the second heretical healer, hailing from Llinger Kingdom and wearing a white uniform."

"Huh? You know me? But more importantly, did you just say 'heretical'?"

He did. I heard him.

The ability to heal wounds was one thing, but my approach—I mean, *Rose's* approach—to using it, that of breaking the body, then mending the body and breaking the body, then mending the body was, well, a pretty twisted use for healing. But thanks to that very approach, I'd become the man I now was.

And okay, even I'll admit it's not exactly normal. Still, I never really thought the information would reach other countries . . .

"I will admit that until I saw it for myself, I was dubious of it." Halpha giggled. "And perhaps that's how most people who live here feel. Compared to the other two, there's a difference in your amount of magic power. Though you have less, you make up for it with purity—it's surprising to see the magic that pulses through your whole body. It is a feat very few are capable of."

"Wait, you can . . . ? Halpha, are you perchance capable of Magical Sight?" asked Welcie, pointing at her own eyes.

Magical Sight? What's that?

"Magical Sight is a type of magic eye," Welcie said, seeing the question marks written all over me. "It allows a person to see the magic power in living things, as well as in the air. It's a rare type of magic not unlike your own, Usato-sama."

"So that's how he knew about us," I stated.

A magic that allowed one to see the flow of magic power. But if his magic was like mine, didn't that mean that Magic Sight was all he had?

Might be too soon to jump to conclusions. I have a feeling that when it comes to this guy, we can't exactly judge the book by its cover.

"Let's pick up the pace a little, shall we?" said Halpha. "The headmistress gave me my orders and I can't be late."

He looked from senpai to Kazuki and then to me, smiled, and took off walking again.

"Usato-kun," said senpai, tapping me on the shoulder as she walked by my side.

I kept an eye on Halpha as I leaned in to hear what she had to say. "I don't like this guy. He's not entirely genuine."

"Ah yes, hatred for one of his own . . . I can see that," I said.

"But Usato-kun, I *am* being genuine."

By the time I realized it, the students around us were gone. All that remained were our footsteps echoing through the corridors. Just as I was admiring the way the corridors were just as spacious as those in Llinger Kingdom, Halpha came to a stop.

"This is the headmistress's office," he said.

He faced the door and knocked politely.

"Headmistress, your guests have arrived," he announced.

After a few moments, we heard a reply.

"Please come in."

Halpha smiled and opened the door.

"After you," he said.

We entered the room. The first thing I noticed was the sunlight streaming into the room.

I had expected an elderly sort of person but was instead faced with a much younger woman than I had imagined. She relaxed in her chair and smiled at us as if she were greeting an old friend.

"Allow me to welcome you all to Luqvist," she said.

I could feel her watching me. That was the first feeling I got—of a strong gaze upon us. The sun pouring in behind her gave her a gentle expression, which, after passing over us, met with Halpha, who stood behind us.

"Thank you, Halpha," she said, her voice ringing with kindness.

"You're welcome. I shall take my leave," he said, bowing and then leaving the room.

"It's nice to meet you," said the woman with a friendly smile. "I am Ira Gladys, the person to whom Luqvist has been entrusted."

So this person governs not just the school, but also the city of Luqvist. And she's so young too. At a glance, she looks like she might be just a bit older than Rose.

"I apologize for the suddenness of our visit," said Welcie. "It has been a long time, Headmistress Gladys."

"It certainly has, hasn't it? I'm glad to see you again, Welcie. Would you be so kind as to let the three children behind you introduce themselves?"

"But of course," said Welcie, taking a step to the side.

So Welcie and Gladys knew each other. Then again, they were both experienced hands in the field of magic—it would have been weirder if they *didn't* know each other. As I was thinking about how they might be acquainted, the heroes and I introduced ourselves.

"Suzune Inukami. It is our honor to meet you."

"Kazuki Ryusen."

"Ken Usato."

"And all of you so full of potential," said Gladys, admiringly. "Though I don't believe you came all this way just to introduce yourselves."

"We did not," said Welcie. "We come today to inform you of the crisis that is fast approaching our continent."

She then took a letter from her person and handed it respectfully to Gladys, who took it in hand and quietly looked over its contents. Though it would have been written in a hurry, ultimately Luqvist was a school for children. With that in mind, the letter was not asking for military cooperation, but other kinds of support. Would they accept its contents, however politely it was written? If it was written like some kind of conscription, explaining the situation could be difficult.

The room fell into a silence so deep that even the sound of the paper rustling seemed deafening. Fear began to build until suddenly Gladys let out a gentle sigh and put the letter on her desk.

"Support against the Demon Lord's army," she said. "I heard that you were victorious in your last battle, no?"

"It was a battle that, for all intents and purposes, we should have lost. That we emerged victorious was only due to the heroes and healer that stand before you and the help of a particular young girl."

Amako. If she hadn't been there, the battle would have been a disaster. The war would have crossed over into truly dangerous territory.

"But I am amazed you would send the heroes themselves. Am I to believe the king is serious about this?"

"Yes. We are painfully aware of how little words can mean on their own."

"Going so far to prove his earnestness. Then again, that *is* one of his merits."

Gladys crossed her arms as she thought, then looked once more at Kazuki and Inukami-senpai.

"Now that I know they're heroes, I can see that they're quite cultured. Well educated, it would seem. After all, they were selected from another world. As for this one," Gladys said, looking at me with some suspicion and confusion, "judging by his uniform, is it safe to say he is one of . . . hers?"

I wasn't surprised by her confusion. There were the two heroes with their special abilities and then me—a healer struggling just to keep up. Gladys's confusion was only natural.

Welcie seemed to sense Gladys's thoughts and jumped in with an explanation.

"Usato is a healer, like Rose. He came from the same world as the heroes. That is the reason that he is here today, also."

Gladys's eyes went wide.

"Hm? Then are you telling me that he's another one?"

"Indeed. Though it may not be obvious from his appearance, Rose has given him her personal stamp of approval."

"Well then. I had wondered, given the similar uniform. But you can't judge a book by its cover, can you?"

Hang on a second. Gladys seems to know about Rose, but me and her, we're different people. I'm not a sadist or the sort of person to watch over people writhing in agony without batting an eyelid.

I wasn't particularly happy about the idea that Gladys might be getting entirely the wrong idea about me. The headmistress put her fingers to her forehead and a stern expression colored her features.

"Given the weight of this request, certainly you understand that this is not a decision I can make on my own. Would you mind waiting for a time? We will need to discuss the matter internally. Or are you in a hurry?"

"We are more than happy to wait until you come to an official decision. We are, after all, making an important request of you," Welcie told her.

"Then please allow me to arrange your accommodation," said Gladys. "You are guests here, and you will be treated as such."

"Your kindness is much appreciated," Welcie said.

I was surprised—everything seemed to be going very smoothly. Luqvist would discuss the matter and prepare a place for us to stay.

I wonder if everything will go as smoothly for me? Probably not, given that my last stop is a place considered unkind to humans.

"So I guess we're just waiting then," whispered Kazuki.

"Nothing else we can do," I replied, relieved.

Maybe it would take a little time, but at least everything was going to plan. As an added bonus, we didn't have to worry about searching for a place to stay. Still, I hadn't been aware of it when we entered, but all the nerves of this first meeting had left me pretty tired. Just then, I saw Gladys take a glossy stone in hand and mutter into it. In the next instant, the door to her office opened and Halpha walked in.

"Halpha," said Gladys, "would you mind arranging accommodation for our guests and showing them to it?"

"As you wish," said Halpha with a bow. "Please follow me, everyone."

We left the office at Halpha's gesture, but not before bowing to Gladys ourselves. Gladys's smile deepened as we did so, and she seemed to remember something.

"Ah, yes," she said. "For the few days you'll be here as we make our decision, perhaps you'd like to see some of the classes here at our school. I'm sure it would be inspiring for our students to be in the presence of ones with such outstanding abilities. That said, it is by no means compulsory."

"Really?! You'll let us do that?!"

As expected, senpai was all in.

"S-Suzune-sama!" said Welcie.

Senpai was over the moon, and Kazuki and I could only chuckle at it. Gladys seemed surprised by senpai's enthusiasm.

"Please, calm down, senpai," I said, taking Inukami-senpai by the arm and dragging her away as she attempted to rush Gladys. "My apologies. She was just as excited even before we got here."

"Wha?! Huh?! Let me go, Usato-kun! Is this who you really are?! The forceful type?!"

"Come along now," I said.

She spoke crazy like this all the time, but there was no need for Gladys to have to know that. And the longer we stayed here, the more likely senpai was to reveal her true self. If at all possible, we wanted Gladys to think of Inukami-senpai in a more favorable light.

"Well then, we'll be excusing ourselves," I said, dragging senpai from the room and following after Halpha.

Kazuki and Welcie seemed wide-eyed as they watched me, but that might have been my imagination. I mean, all I'd done was drag the instinctively loyal Inukami-senpai out of the room.

"Kazuki-sama," said Welcie. "Perhaps it would be wisest to let Usato-sama take care of Suzune-sama from now on."

"You make a good point. I think that's for the best."

Come on, guys. Don't make me do this on my own.

"Hmph," said senpai. "A wonderful idea. Consider me fully on board."

"I am going to throw you out of the school grounds," I muttered.

And why was she agreeing with them, anyway?

* * *

The accommodation that Halpha brought us to was practically next door to the school proper. According to him, Gladys had already considered our accompanying knights and had readied rooms for our whole party. I was happy to hear that Aruku and the others would be able to rest and relax. They'd spent the whole of this journey focused on our protection. I'd spent our breaks healing their exhaustion with my magic, but there was nothing I could do about their mental weariness. I hoped they could use these few days to relax both their minds and their bodies.

Anyway, now that our accommodation was all set, it was time to move on to what needed handling next. We would need to move our luggage at some point, but my first priority was to help out Amako. So once I made sure senpai and Kazuki had gone into our lodging, I called out to Welcie.

"I'm going to tell Aruku and the other knights about this place," I told her. "And also . . . thank you for doing all of that for us today."

Welcie smiled awkwardly. She seemed almost apologetic for it.

"This is truly nothing at all," she said. "It's certainly much harder for you than it is for me."

"Well, you can say that, but I chose to accept it," I said. "And besides, I feel like I owe it to the Llinger Kingdom for treating me so well."

"Suzune-sama and Kazuki-sama both said the same thing," said Welcie, still looking apologetic about it all.

I finally realized then that Welcie still harbored some feelings of guilt within her because it was her who had summoned the three of us to this world. After everything we'd been through, we'd come to terms with it. Kazuki, Inukami-senpai, and I—none of us harbored any ill will toward the people of Llinger Kingdom. They had their own unavoidable reasons for summoning us, and they treated us very well for it.

"I'm really glad that I met you and all the other people I've encountered since I got here," I said. "I got to make friends with a cool guy like Kazuki and a pretty girl like Inukami-senpai. That's more than enough for me."

"You . . . you probably shouldn't say that in front of Suzune-sama," Welcie said.

"Yeah, that's true. I guess it's our secret then."

Welcie giggled.

"My lips are sealed."

Her smile relaxed and the guilt seemed to dissipate from her voice. I *really* hoped she wouldn't say anything to senpai though. I'd said too much for a guy like me—I felt like I was putting on an act, like I was selling myself like a playboy.

"Okay, well, I'll be off then," I said.

"See you when you return."

I felt suddenly less bold than I had earlier, and I turned from Welcie shamefully. After what I'd already said, I figured I shouldn't play more into the character. I always ended up feeling kind of embarrassed like this. I felt myself blushing as I headed back the way we'd come, for the gates.

It was nearing dusk, and there were far fewer people on the streets. The main streets were more relaxed as I walked them.

I noticed a group of robed people heading toward an alley. Among them was the boy I'd seen when we first arrived. I couldn't see his face because he had his head down, but something didn't feel right.

I got curious, so I peeked into the alley into which they'd all turned. At the end of it was another square, not unlike a park. There was a group of robed students there casting magic from the palms of their hands, chatting, and laughing. The boy I'd met earlier simply watched the magic casting with no expression, but there was nothing particularly out of the ordinary about it. Outside of the magic, in fact, it looked just like any other park from my home world.

"Maybe I was just imagining things," I said.

I'd prepared myself to see bullying or something like it, but it seemed like my worries were entirely misplaced. Most likely, I was just on edge because that beastkin girl had attacked me earlier.

I headed back to the main road and got to walking again. That boy was different to the other kids. His robe was dirty with soot. The other kids were about the same age as Amako, and their robes were pristine. The difference wasn't anything more than that, but I just couldn't seem to let it go.

Something bothered me.

Then again, maybe I shouldn't go poking my nose into what isn't my business. I don't want to get pulled into anything that'll get me in trouble.

The topic filled my thoughts until I reached the gates. I found Aruku and Amako near the stables, where the carriage was. I was glad to see Blurin looking peacefully calm too. I waved at them.

"Sir Usato!" called Aruku, waving back when he saw me.

I mentally ran over everything we'd been through so I could summarize it for Aruku. I gave him the rundown.

"Ah, the lodging in front of the school. Yes, I know the place," said Aruku.

Surprisingly enough, I didn't have to explain very much.

"There's no need to worry about us," said Aruku with a smile. "I already know the way to the lodging, so you and Amako are free to visit her friends. I'm sure it's been a long time and she'll want to see them as soon as possible."

This guy . . . nothing if not considerate.

"Thank you so much, Aruku," I said. "Come on, Amako. You say thanks too."

"Thank you . . . Sir . . . Aruku."

Come to think of it, why doesn't she ever call me "sir"? I mean, I'm older than her, right?

I leaned down to ask, but she spoke before I could say anything.

"It's too embarrassing to call you 'sir,'" she said.

"Wait, what does that mean?"

Is she talking about how much she likes me? Or does she mean that she doesn't want to call me "sir"? I wish she'd be a little clearer.

Aruku chuckled.

"I'll leave two people here to watch over things, so if anything happens, feel free to let them know. We'll take care of Blurin too," Aruku confirmed.

"Thank you so much for all of this, Aruku. Alright then, let's get going, shall we, Amako?"

"Okay," said the beastkin. "It's this way."

Aruku was so reliable. He was the very definition of the word.

With Amako leading me by the hand, we walked through town. She was bright and happy, and I could see her tail wagging underneath her white cloak.

"Oh, right," I said, suddenly remembering that I had to tell Amako about the beastkin that had attacked me earlier in the day. "Amako? I should probably tell you about something before we meet up with your friend."

"They live nearby, so we'll get to them soon. I can't wait to introduce you!"

"Yeah, wait, about that . . ."

She was so happy I couldn't have slowed her down even if I'd tried.

If the person we were going to meet was the same girl who punched me, there was a chance she might attack me on sight. As I was wracking my brain for what to do, we left the wide main street for a narrow alleyway. It scared me how dark it suddenly got, and then Amako suddenly came to a stop.

"Here it is," she said.

In front of us was a run-down house with a hint of light leaking from its windows. It didn't look like it was going to crumble anytime soon, but the dark atmosphere gave it a creepy vibe.

Are there people seriously living here?

"It's easier for us to live in places like this," said Amako.

"Oh, I see."

Nobody willingly chose to live in a dank, creepy place like this. That explained the location and the appearance. Still, it bothered me that the area was so deserted. This afternoon, the girl hadn't been going full power, but there was every chance that, this time, she might come at me with everything she had.

"Amako," I said, "if I'm here, I'll just get in the way of you catching up with your friends after so long. So you just go have fun without me. I'm happy just seeing you happy."

"What are you talking about? You should meet them too. Don't make excuses . . . I don't mind at all if you're here . . . No, you won't get in the way . . . You're being weird, Usato . . . Are you hiding something?"

"Look at you, just shutting down our conversation so naturally before we can even have it," I said. "You already know everything I wanted to say."

It was like she was reading my mind, except she was reading the future. She could see the conversations we would conceivably have. It usually made things easier—she took away the work of actually having the conversation. But because she could see what I was going to say, she could shut down my excuses before I could say them. I'd never win an argument against her in my life.

If I could use prescience, I'd get back at Rose by . . . Wait, that wouldn't work. It doesn't work physically.

"Fine, fine," I said, giving up. "Here's the deal . . ."

I told Amako all about what happened earlier in the day. When I described what the beastkin girl looked like, she matched the person that Amako wanted me to meet. It wasn't what Amako wanted to hear, and she was even more shocked that I'd been punched.

"Okay, I understand," said Amako. "You stand behind me, and I'll clear things up."

"Look at me," I said, sighing, "hiding behind a girl so much younger than me."

Amako stood in front of me and knocked on the door of the house. At first, there was nothing. Then Amako suddenly shivered where she stood and leaped to the side without even saying a word.

Huh? Why would she jump like that?

"So you found out where I live, huh, monster?!"

Just as Amako jumped out of the way, the door burst open with a kick and someone leaped out at me with a broom in hand.

"Oh . . . *now* I get it," I said.

I could see where this was going because of the voice, which I recognized, and the broom that came swinging for me. I let out a sigh and cast healing magic around myself. I could tell immediately by the burning rage in the girl's almond-shaped eyes that she wasn't about to listen to reason.

So Amako dodged out of the way to avoid this, huh? That makes sense, but I wish she could have said something to me.

I stepped out of the way of the incoming broom and put some distance between myself and my attacker. The girl was up in arms, poking her broom toward me menacingly.

"I don't know what kind of monster you are," she said, "but I won't let you touch anybody here!"

"Okay," I said, "let's hold up a minute. First, a correction, if I may. I'm human. Take a look. I'm no different from other humans, right?"

I know it was weird, but that's what happened—I started off by proving that I was, indeed, human. But the girl only glared at me, as if she wasn't about to let herself get fooled so easily.

"What else could you be except some kind of human-shaped ogre with regenerative abilities?! Calling yourself human?! You think I'm stupid?! I know the difference between humans and monsters!"

A human-shaped ogre with regenerative abilities? How hurtful can you get? She's talking like I'm some kind of test subject that escaped from the lab.

I felt anger welling inside me, but I cooled my heart, put on the best smile I possibly could, and tried to reason with her.

"You realize there's a thing called politeness, right? You realize it's not very nice to call people monsters and ogres, right? You shouldn't go around throwing those names at people."

It's like she's talking about Rose and all the members of the Rescue Team. Oh wait, they are *monsters, so she wouldn't be wrong.*

I elected to ignore the uncomfortable direction those thoughts were leaning in and put my efforts into amicably ironing out my misunderstanding with this beastkin girl. Based on her reaction, however, it seemed near impossible.

Come on, Amako. This is where you're supposed to jump in! Wait, why does she look so petrified of me? And the beastkin girl too, she's backing away in terror!

"F-Finally you reveal your true self!" she shouted.

What now? I am cooler and calmer than I ever have been. Ah-ha. Perhaps I'm not smiling enough. Weird. This is about as smiley as I get, and those two are totally on guard.

"What's wrong?"

It didn't seem like Amako could get me out of this. And this beastkin girl was refusing to listen to reason. Everything I did was like fuel to the fire.

"Guess I don't have a choice," I muttered, sending healing magic throughout my body and concentrating it into my fists. "If you won't listen, then I'll just have to make you."

I would calm her down with a kind and gentle Healing Punch. Nobody would get hurt, and we'd all be able to talk through this misunderstanding.

For some reason, the beastkin girl let out a gasp and took another step back. But I wasn't about to let this standstill between us go on any longer.

So first things first—I have to take that broom of hers and break it.

"Here we go," I said.

I took a step forward, ready to close the distance in an instant. Then I kicked off the floor and sped toward the beastkin girl, my fist pulled back.

"Usato! Stop!" cried Amako, sliding between me and the beastkin girl.

Her sudden entrance was a shock, but I did what she said and put on the brakes. She held both hands out toward me with a reproving look on her face.

"Stop. Calm down. Come back to your senses," she said.

Why does she look like she's trying to calm some kind of wild beast?

"Huh? But I am calm," I said.

"Then what about that fist?"

"I just figured that I would calm her down with it, that's all."

"Maybe you can heal a bruise with that thing, but you'll still scar a person's heart."

How does she see me in this moment? I was never going to traumatize the girl. Well, that wasn't my intention, anyway.

"The scariest thing is that you don't even see it yourself," said Amako.

"Hm?"

"Never mind. Leave the rest to me."

Well, okay. I guess I can just let Amako handle things now.

With Amako between us, even the beastkin girl had calmed down.

"Wait," she uttered, a look of disbelief rising to her face. "Th-That voice . . . Amako?"

She let her broom clatter to the ground.

"Kiriha," said Amako, removing the hood of her cloak. "Long time no see!"

Her face was now clearly visible—her golden hair and triangular foxlike ears as clear as day. Amako glanced in my direction and then turned back to the girl called Kiriha.

"This guy is not your enemy," she said, reassuring her friend, "and he's human. Mostly."

Mostly?! What does that mean?!

"I'm so sorry! I had completely the wrong idea!" Kiriha said.

Kiriha and I had finally cleared the air, but that didn't exactly make things any easier. I was traveling with Amako because there was a chance I could help her mother, but Kiriha hadn't just gotten things mixed up; she'd also straight up attacked me. She was very harsh on herself about it. Even I was cringing at the extent of it.

She was on her knees in front of me, apologizing profusely. It made me feel all kinds of awkward. At the same time, I was pretty shocked—I didn't know this kind of deep *dogeza*-style apology existed outside of my own world.

"Don't worry, Usato doesn't mind," said Amako. "He's a bit scary sometimes, but he's a good person. It's just . . . he can be scary sometimes."

"Hey," I said, "why did you need to say that part twice?"

Amako ignored me.

"But I can't believe I did that to you," said Kiriha.

"Amako is going overboard about the scary stuff, but really, don't worry about it. I know you had your own reasons for doing what you did, and as you can see, I'm completely unharmed."

I knelt in front of Kiriha and showed her my hand, where she'd punched me earlier in the day. Thanks to my healing magic, there wasn't even a scar. Kiriha lifted herself up and took my hand in her own, looking at it carefully. She let out an awed sigh.

"I've seen healing magic before, but this is something else entirely. Not even a scratch!"

"You know another healer?" I asked.

"He's useless compared to you."

Useless?

I wanted to ask more about it, but Kiriha stood to her feet. I decided I could ask more later.

In any case, I hadn't come here so that Kiriha would apologize to me. I'd come so that Amako could meet up with her friends. With that in mind, I wanted to forget all about something as trivial as me being attacked as soon as possible.

"I'm doing my best to understand the way beastkin people see humans," I said. "That's why I don't think it's crazy that you thought I might have ulterior motives. Same with you attacking me. And I could have been clearer up front, too. Let's call it even."

It was true that I'd been too thoughtless. There was no need for me to even take Kiriha's punch in the first place. I could have tried reasoning with her more. I think it was likely that I just wanted to try out my skills after all the training I'd been through. But I was still immature and a long way from being what Rose expected of me.

Kiriha was slack-jawed in shock at my words. So shocked that she laughed.

"You are a weird one, that's for sure. And to think I was so terrified of what you might demand in terms of reparations. Then again, I guess I should have expected more from someone that Amako brought with her. Still, you really are . . . a weird human."

"My eyes see true," said Amako.

"I guess they really do, don't they?" said Kiriha with another laugh as she wiped the dust from her clothes and tail.

She wasn't wearing her usual robe. I guessed that was because she was at home. Instead, Kiriha wore some plain and simple clothes. Her ears and tail were completely unhidden. Kiriha's tail was mostly white with some brown at the tip. She didn't look like a fox or a dog-type beastkin. I didn't know what she was. I thought maybe she was an itachi because of the whirlwind cutting stuff, but I couldn't say for certain.

I just knew I couldn't introduce Inukami-senpai to her. Inukami'd go wild.

"Usato, staring is rude," said Amako. "Especially the way you're staring."

"Hm? Oh, sorry. I didn't mean anything by it."

"He really is a weird one, isn't he?" remarked Kiriha. "Most humans see me and react with disgust."

But I'm not from around here. And in my world, there are lots of people who love cute animal-human hybrids. I think it's safe to say there actually aren't many people who hate them.

As I was lost in these mundane thoughts, Kiriha walked up to me and put out her hand. When our eyes met, she scratched her cheek somewhat bashfully.

A simple handshake, right? Please tell me it's not some cultural thing I don't understand like a one-hand-shake-to-the-death-match.

I reached out and took her hand, and though she looked surprised at first, we shook hands.

"I still haven't introduced myself, have I?" she said. "I'm Kiriha, a senior here at the school."

"I'm Usato. I'm a healer and a member of the Llinger Kingdom Rescue Team. I guess this handshake makes us friends now, right?"

Kiriha laughed.

"Works for me."

With that out of the way, it seemed like finally Amako and Kiriha could speak freely and easily.

"Oh, I just remembered. I was right in the middle of preparing dinner. My little brother should be home soon. Would you like to have dinner with us? Consider it part of my apology."

"Dinner, huh?" I said.

They'll be serving dinner at the lodging that Gladys prepared for us. I don't want to make Kiriha's brother feel awkward, and besides, it might be easier for all of them to catch up without me around.

"Um . . . I should probably . . . Hm? Huh?"

Amako was pulling at the sleeve of my coat. She looked up at me with a pleading look in her eyes.

"Have dinner with us," she pleaded.

"Well, now I don't have a choice, do I?"

I just couldn't say no to the girl. Perhaps because I'd heard about how hard life was on her recently, I didn't want her to have to feel that loneliness again. Once Kiriha saw our back-and-forth, she seemed especially enthusiastic about making enough for me too. There was no backing out anymore, that was for sure.

"You don't have to worry about feeling like you're causing us any trouble," said Kiriha. "Now, I know it won't be anything too luxurious, but I'm going to treat you two to a feast!"

She lifted the door she had kicked down earlier and ushered us into the house. Inside, it reminded me a lot of the Rescue Team dorms. It wasn't particularly spacious, but in the room that we entered, there was a table large enough for ten and stairs leading up to a second floor.

"Nice place," I said.

"Are you being sarcastic, or do you really mean that?" Kiriha asked.

"I live in a really similar place back at Llinger Kingdom," I explained. "I honestly think it's a nice place. Makes me feel at home."

I wonder how Felm is doing? Is she making sure to eat properly? She's probably still slacking off and still getting beaten up by Rose, I imagine. She is the newest recruit after me though, so I pray she's at least safe.

"What are you spacing out for, Usato?" asked Amako.

"Oh, uh . . . it's nothing."

I glanced at Kiriha behind us, who leaned the front door back against the frame, then walked to where the tables and chairs were. Steam wafted from further back in the room—the kitchen, perhaps.

"I guess I went a little too far," said Kiriha, laughing, "kicking the door down and all."

"You've always been like that," said Amako. "Act first, think later. You almost hit me with that kick, actually. Well, the door hit me a little."

"I'm sorry, I'm sorry. I'm going to make dinner, so you two feel free to just take a seat and relax. I won't be long."

Unable to stand up to Amako's reproachful stare, Kiriha escaped to the kitchen. It made me chuckle. I took a seat at the table and let out a breath. Amako sat down next to me. It looked like that was where she used to sit when she lived here, because she ran her hands along the wooden table—there was a hint of nostalgia in the gesture.

"I'm glad I could bring you here, Amako," I said.

"All thanks to you, Usato."

"Little too early for thanks. I still haven't saved your mother yet."

"Yeah, but still. Thanks."

Whenever she had that gentle expression on her face, I never knew what to do. However indirectly, Amako had saved countless lives when she warned me of the destruction of the kingdom and the death of my friends. And thanks to her, I had a place to go home to when the battle had ended. A place to go with my friends and companions.

If anyone should have been saying thanks, it was me.

"You saved my friends, and you saved countless lives," I said. "So I'm just returning the favor. To the best of my ability, anyway."

"The best of your ability . . . You *are* warped, Usato."

She was saying it the same way Kazuki and Inukami-senpai said it back when we were in the carriage on the way here. She was also smiling in a way she usually didn't.

"I am not," I protested. "I told you—this is normal."

Wait a second. Wasn't Amako asleep while we were having that discussion?

"Finally, you decide to smile and it's because of something like this? It's like *you're* going to warp me."

"Any more than you already are and you'll be in big trouble."

Rub it in, why don't you.

Compared to the gloomy and downtrodden girl she was when we first met, Amako was brighter now than I ever thought possible. It made me happy. Now, what could I do to somehow catch her off guard?

I knew that because she could see the future, ordinary conversation was meaningless. I had to be thinking of conversations many steps ahead. I was just about to try out my plan and talk to Amako, but she was looking at the broken front door of the house. When I turned to look myself, I realized there was someone standing there.

"Man, am I hungry," said the person, a young beastkin boy. "Also, uh . . . why is the door bashed open? Wha?! Who are you?!"

He was a little taller than me, with the same features as Kiriha. The moment I entered his field of vision, he spread his legs wide and faced me as he would an enemy. He wore the same sort of greaves on his legs as Kiriha did on her hands. I was over getting attacked for the day, so I immediately gave up before we got into anything either of us would regret.

"Wait!" I said, doing everything in my power to exude a threat level of zero. "Wait, I'm here with Amako. I'm safe! I'm not suspicious or anything!"

If I could at all avoid it, I didn't want to get hurt. I was used to pain, but it wasn't like that made it go away.

"What?! Amako?! If you're going to lie, at least . . . do a . . . better . . ."

The boy was running to attack me when he noticed Amako behind me. His ears stood at attention and a look of surprise filled his face.

"Amako!" he cried, pointing at her. "You're alive!"

The boy's eyes looked like they might pop from his head. In contrast, Amako raised a hand quite casually.

"Yep. Long time no see. This guy here is not an enemy."

"Not an enemy . . . but he's so shady!"

"I know, I know . . . but you shouldn't say mean things about him."

Should I assume she's defending me by saying that? I finally discovered healing magic's weak point. It doesn't work on the heart. I can handle all sorts of abuse, and I've even gotten used to it, but these casual insults still sting so bad. But still . . . shady? I really like this uniform.

The boy's name was Kyo, and just like Kiriha, he wilted under Amako's reproachful stare. I didn't expect him to trust me as quickly as Kiriha—his attitude seemed to have deeper roots. Still, I wasn't here to boost his mood or anything like that, so it wasn't a huge problem. What was more important was whether I could get them to look after Amako while we were here. She'd be much more comfortable here among friends than at the lodging we were provided, and I could tell by Kyo's angry and unceasing glare that he and Kiriha both worried about her. If they were looking after her, I wouldn't have to worry.

"Oh, so is this the healer that Amako was looking for? But he's so thin and he looks so fragile. Are you sure that you'll be okay?"

Kyo made an odd criticism, perhaps because he didn't like me much. I didn't feel especially like I should argue back, so I stayed silent. Amako dropped into a pout and was about to say something when Kiriha did instead.

"There's nothing to worry about, Kyo," she said as she brought food from the kitchen in both hands. "He's nothing like the healer we know."

"What?!"

"This is my twin brother, Kyo," said Kiriha. "I didn't expect him to come home *quite* so early. Otherwise, I could've prepared for his outburst."

We were all sitting around the table eating the food Kiriha had made. Kyo and I had been introduced to each other now, but he still didn't seem to like me much. He sat across the table from me, next to his sister, stuffing bread into his mouth as he glared at me.

I don't get it. We've been properly introduced, and Kiriha cleared the air so there's no misunderstanding. Why's he still looking at me like I'm his enemy?

"Come on, Kyo," said Kiriha. "I know you're worried about Amako, but quit it with the evil eye treatment."

"Don't you think this guy looks shady though?"

"I did at first, sure. But Amako trusts him, and he's completely different from other humans we've met. He reached out to shake my hand even knowing that I'm a beastkin. He's not even creeped out by the ears and the tail. He didn't even demand reparations for our scuffle. Weird, right?"

Kiriha said all of this quite happily. I guess I was a rarity of sorts. All the same, Kyo's glare told me he still didn't trust me.

Why is this guy lashing out at me, anyway? Does he have a thing for Amako? I mean, maybe he does. Besides her being kind of cheeky of late, she is *cute, that's for sure.*

I glanced at Amako by my side and let out a sigh as I spooned some soup into my mouth.

"Hm? Wow, this soup," I said, smacking my lips, "it's good."

It was simple and gentle like a potato soup and salted just right. Kiriha's eyes went wide at my words and she laughed.

"I've never been complimented by a human before. You really are weird."

So she's surprised when I praise her soup, and all I get for it is being called weird again. I don't understand beastkin table manners at all.

I was just about to spoon some more soup into my mouth when Kyo leaped to his feet.

"I know this healer isn't like the other humans I know. I will give him that much. But!" he declared, staring at me with a stronger glare than before. "You better watch out if you even think about doing anything to Amako or my big sister!"

I didn't know what had happened to Kyo here in Luqvist, but I knew it was reason enough for him to have a strong distrust of humans.

And if that's the case, I probably shouldn't stick around. I should get my business over with and get out of here.

"To be honest with you," I said, "I don't care if you trust me or not."

"What?!"

"I'm here with Amako today because I wanted to ask if you could take care of her while we're here in Luqvist."

"Oh? Really?" asked Amako.

Amako, I thought you knew this already.

I ignored the blank look of surprise on Amako's face and met Kyo's eyes, still staring at me with suspicion. He seemed to feel awkward with my eyes on him, so he looked away. He shut his mouth and kept it closed as I turned to Kiriha.

"Kiriha, would you mind looking after Amako while we're here in Luqvist? I think she'd enjoy being here much more than she would with me and my traveling party, and she'd be much more at ease."

"But of course! We've got a spare room and enough money to feed an extra mouth or two."

"What a relief."

It wouldn't be for a long time, but I felt sure Amako would prefer staying with other beastkin instead of with a group of humans. Not to mention the fact that we were considered guests of the state, meaning we'd draw attention to ourselves even if we tried to avoid it. It might cause trouble if Amako was spotted in and amongst all of that. We didn't mind the attention, per se, but perhaps some of the less civil types in town would try to kidnap her or something.

"In that case," said Kiriha, "I'll ready things for an extra two."

I have a good feeling I can leave things in Kiriha's hands. She'll protect Amako, and with those two around, I can . . . Wait. Huh?

"Two?" I asked.

Who is she counting as the second?

"Huh?" asked Kiriha, puzzled. "Aren't you staying too?"

"What?"

I was so surprised it was the only word I could muster. I couldn't understand how she had interpreted my words as to think I would be staying too.

"Kiriha! No! Way! Letting that guy stay?! Here?! It's a bad idea!" the brother went on.

Kyo leaped to his feet again, this time speaking on my behalf.

Yeah, you tell her, Kyo! Tell her what I can't!

"No, no, it's better if they're both here together," Kiriha said, shrugging him off. "You don't have to worry about a thing. If he was going to do something—anything—he would have done it already. Right, Amako?"

Kiriha looked at Amako, and Kyo did the same.

"A-Amako?" he asked, his voice trembling.

Amako looked up at me hesitantly.

"As long as it's okay with you, Usato . . ." she said.

No way!

I was so shocked she'd say such a thing that I dropped my spoon.

How are you supposed to relax around Kiriha and Kyo with me around?! Are you sure that's what you want?

"Well, you heard her," said Kiriha with a grin. "How about it, Usato?"

Kyo wouldn't look at me. Amako had gone back to eating her dinner.

What is this? Why do I feel like I'm being pushed into a corner?

As long as it's okay with me? What am I supposed to say to that?

"I'll have to let the knights know about this so they can tell the others," I said.

I might be weak under this kind of pressure, but Amako looks happy, so I guess it doesn't matter.

I could see her ears wavering happily, so I decided just to go with the flow and stay with Kiriha and Kyo.

* * *

It was a building at the edges of Luqvist. It was our home. It was the place my beastkin seniors had shown me when we first got here. At first, I thought that there'd be people among all the humans who would accept us. After all, Luqvist is a big city where tens of thousands of people gather. There had to be some people, however few, who were generous and kind-hearted toward our species. That was the hope that I held in my heart when I left the hidden village we called home and went to Luqvist to master magic.

I wanted to learn. My people had told me I had a talent for magic. I also wanted to make friends with people outside of the village.

But it was not long after arriving in Luqvist that I realized my hopes were those of a fool. On the surface, the city had banned oppression against demi-humans, so for all intents and purposes, it was never seen. But in its place was an ever-present, aching solitude from all directions.

Distrust. Contempt. Fear.

Friendship was impossible.

Solitude was forced upon us.

The only way to show my worth as a beastkin mage wasn't through friendship or influence—there was only one way, and that was magic power.

I was made to understand that Luqvist was the best environment for polishing one's magic and skills. People could achieve harmony among one another, but to them, the beastkin weren't people. I was stared at by so many, as if I was a freak, that it crushed me with sadness. The other beastkin in Luqvist kept to themselves. They stayed away from humans. They didn't try to adjust. They didn't trust anyone.

They weren't weak, like I was. They could stand being alone in a way that I couldn't.

The others kept to themselves and devoted themselves to magic. They stayed on guard, and they expected nothing of humans. That was who they were.

But when I looked at them, I thought . . . Or more accurately, when I looked at them, I couldn't help but think, *Perhaps I should have done things differently.*

When did it start to happen? When did I start hiding my ears out in public? When did it get to the point that I focused entirely on developing my magical skills?

There's no point being here if you aren't powerful. We're not here to make friends with humans.

Words I repeated to myself as the two of us, my brother and I, stayed in that lonely house of ours. I thought that over and over. And then one day, a beastkin girl arrived in town. She was not from a hidden village, like us. She was from the Beastlands, where hatred for humans was especially strong. And she had the strange ability to read the future. Her name was Amako.

She told us that she was in search of a healer and that she had come a long, long way in the hope of saving her mother. Healing is a magic that only humans can use, so I thought it a fool's errand, because cooperating with humans was impossible. And true enough, Luqvist's own healer had already turned her away.

"Kiriha, I will not give up," Amako had said.

And she didn't. She wanted to save her mother, and she would keep searching even if it meant putting herself in danger. Coming as far as Luqvist was dangerous enough. She had already faced countless dangers. Kyo had tried to stop her, right up until the end, but I couldn't bring myself to do the same.

Could I work as hard as Amako did?

Could I try to trust in humans?

Did humans who could get along with beastkin even exist?

I did not have an answer.

The answer had been there for so long, and yet I couldn't seem to believe it was true. Perhaps I still feel that way. Perhaps I still feel as though a human will arrive who can be friends with a beastkin like me.

"Morning?"

I woke to the sounds of the morning bells. I felt the traces of an old dream, but I couldn't remember what it was. I just knew that half of it was stuff I'd rather forget. I got up off the stiff bed and took to my tail with my hands. Once it was brushed, I got changed and left my room to ready breakfast.

The living room was right outside of my room, but today something was different. I could hear voices outside.

Who would be making such a racket at this hour of the morning? If it's the neighbors, then I'll have to say something to them.

I shifted the door I'd broken to the side and peeked outside. I was not prepared for the odd sight that met my eyes.

"You're way too light, Amako! I can't train at all like this!"

"That's not my fault, Usato."

"Fair enough. I guess I just have to keep working until you *feel* heavy!"

Usato was doing push-ups. Amako was sitting on his back. From the looks of things, he was doing some kind of morning training routine. Still, it was anything but ordinary.

Usato was on one hand, moving rhythmically up and down at a speed way faster than anyone would consider normal. He never slowed down, and he never looked tired. Sometimes he even joked with Amako. It was like the training was nothing to him. It gave me the creeps.

Why is this human doing push-ups so early in the morning? And why is Amako just riding his back like it's nothing at all?

It was quite a shocking sight to wake up to, so I slid the door back in place before they noticed, took a deep breath, and went to the kitchen to prepare breakfast. Once there, I started getting ingredients together. Then I remembered what Usato had said at dinner the night before.

"Delicious . . ." I muttered.

That was what he'd called it. He'd called my soup delicious. I wasn't usually the type to be so naively swayed by such words, but they certainly were a surprise. I'd told Kyo that he could trust Usato then, but to be honest, I still didn't completely trust him myself. That was why I'd acted like everything was fine, and then I'd sat across from him and fed him food I made. Food made by a beastkin. No ordinary human would ever eat food prepared by a beastkin, let alone call it delicious.

"All talk, no action. That's me, huh?"

I know he'd healed himself afterward, but the truth of the matter was that I'd still injured him, and quite badly at that. Then I'd said all kinds of nasty things to him. But then he forgave me. I felt awful that, even then, I still just couldn't trust him.

"Oh, right. Breakfast," I muttered, remembering that I had to go and wake Kyo up.

If I took too long making breakfast, we'd be late for class. I'd decided to make a proper breakfast, but I had to make it quick.

Once breakfast was ready, I sat at the table with Usato, Amako, and Kyo, who had just woken up. Usato was a little late on account of working up a sweat, but it felt like a long time since I'd had such a busy breakfast.

"Watch yourself!" said Kyo, who was getting ready to go to school. "You do anything weird to my sister and you're going to get it!"

Usato just stood there drinking water and scratching his cheek, unsure of what to do. I couldn't help but laugh at my overprotective little brother and decided to help Usato out a little.

"Look at the time, Kyo. You know your teacher this morning doesn't stand for tardy students, so you better get a move on, no?"

Kyo's face went pale.

"What?! Is it that time already?" he said, throwing his bag on his shoulder and speeding for the door. "I'm outta here!"

"See you later!"

Usato watched him disappear in the direction of the city, then turned toward me, a look of confusion on his face.

"Kiriha, you and Kyo are twins, right? If you're the same age, don't you take the same classes?"

"Oh . . ." I said, realizing what he meant. It was a good question. "We take the same basic classes, but some of our classes are separate too. At Luqvist, some subjects are made compulsory, but the rest are free for students to choose as they like. Kyo and I take different elective classes when it comes to our interests."

"Oh, so it's like a university."

I didn't know what a *university* was, but it was probably the same as the Luqvist school system.

"My teacher tends to be pretty easygoing when it comes to time, but Kyo's teacher is a bit on the eccentric side—it's pretty troublesome if you end up late for class."

"Ah, I see. So that means you'll go to school soon too?"

"Yep . . . What about you two? Are you going to hang out here?"

"No, I'll head to the stables by the gates to meet up with the people we came with. Are you coming too, Amako?"

"Yep."

It seemed like Amako trusted him, so at least I didn't have to worry about her. At the same time, I knew they couldn't spend all day wandering around town, so I made a mental note to come home early.

"I wonder what I should make for dinner?" I muttered as I washed the dishes.

"Oh, and thanks for the change of clothes," said Usato, who had changed into clothes similar to his white coat. "I washed them before breakfast and hung them outside but . . . are you sure it's okay?"

"Don't worry about it. It's nothing. I just loaned you some of Kyo's clothes."

I looked outside and found the clothes neatly hung outside, just like he said. He was quite polite and well-mannered like that. It was an odd contrast to the terrifying face he'd worn just one day previously. It was truly frightening. Maybe calling him an ogre was going too far, but who put on faces like that? It was the first time I'd ever felt completely overwhelmed by a human face.

"You look a bit pale," said Amako. "You feeling okay?"

"Oh. Uh, yes. I'm fine. Just fine."

Those feelings must have been showing on *my* face.

Didn't you ask Amako all about him last night? You know he's not a bad person. And you know that Llinger Kingdom—where she spent two years—is a much, much nicer place than you ever imagined.

I plunged my trembling hands into the cold water to calm myself down. Just as I was feeling like I was coming back to my senses, Usato poked his head into the kitchen.

"Well then, we'll get going," he said.

"We'll see you later, Kiriha," said Amako.

The two of them wore white hooded coats, and at least to me, they looked like completely ordinary friends. I'd long thought that such a friendship was completely impossible, no matter how much you wanted it, and yet it was right there in front of my eyes. I felt feelings welling up in me that I couldn't put words to.

"Okay," I said with a forced laugh. "I'll see you later."

There was no energy left in my voice, and I must have looked worried. Usato tilted his head curiously, but Amako definitely knew something was up. Even without her prescience, she was sharp, and she was bright.

"I guess I'll start getting ready to head out too," I said.

I was finally reunited with the friend I'd longed to see. And yet, for some strange reason, there was no joy in my heart.

* * *

"A message from senpai?"

When we got to the stables after leaving Kiriha's house, the knight on guard duty had a message for me. It was the same knight I'd asked to pass a message for me yesterday afternoon, and it seemed that she'd given him one in return.

"Yes," said the knight. "They ask that you join them when you come back to town."

"So their lodging then?"

"Indeed."

I'd been planning to do that anyway, but I was kind of afraid of how senpai would react. She could be childish like that. I just hoped she wasn't sulking or sullen about anything.

"Maybe something came up," I said to Amako. "Knowing her, she probably knew that I would be here early in the morning, so I should go meet her and Kazuki first."

I also had to explain to them why I'd suddenly changed the place where I was staying without telling them in person.

"Amako, will you look after Blurin for me?" I asked.

"Sure thing. I don't mind being around him at all," she said, kneeling down and rubbing the grizzly's nose as he happily munched on some fruit. At least this way Amako wouldn't be bored by herself. And she had knights to protect her in case anything happened too.

"Alright then, I'm going to meet up with the heroes. Look after Amako, okay?"

"Understood," said the knight. "Travel safe!"

I took off at a light run, heading for the lodge in front of the school of magic. It was only a few minutes away if I ran. I'd gotten a feel for the distance yesterday, and it was all pretty smooth so long as I didn't get caught in the crowds.

"The city center, huh?" I muttered. "There are differences, but it still reminds me of Llinger Kingdom."

As I ran through the streets, I couldn't help wanting to do as I did in Llinger Kingdom and go on a jog with heavy weights. I hadn't brought any weights with me, which meant I could only really do regular jogging.

Then again, I do have Blurin so . . . No, that wouldn't work. Everyone here would be way too shocked.

"Maybe I can ask Gladys for help?" I said to myself.

I only had knowledge of the things I'd read in books, but I knew of creatures called "familiars" in this world that acted like servants for people. So maybe there was a chance Gladys would give me permission to go running with Blurin. I didn't know if our relationship was the same as a familiar-master relationship, but it was at least worth asking.

In terms of weight, Blurin is just right, so I'd love to go running with him if that's an option.

"This place . . ." I began.

I hadn't been thinking about it before, but now I realized that I'd made it to the alleyway I found the previous day where the group of students went. I was going to pass on by, but then I saw a crowd of people at the other end and got curious.

"Did something happen?" I asked myself.

They all look like bystanders, so it sure seems that way.

My curiosity got the better of me and I decided to check out the commotion before heading to the lodge. As I got closer, I could hear people talking.

"Yeah, it was them again. I can't believe they'd do such a thing."

"I mean, they could just leave him alone."

"I don't want to get pulled into it. That would be awful."

It was all very ominous, and I felt a bad feeling creeping up in me as I pushed through the crowd. When I got to the front, I was shocked by what I saw.

It was a boy in the dirty robe. He'd collapsed on the road, and he looked beaten up.

Wait, I know this boy. He'd entered the alleyway with that group yesterday.

I ran up to the boy and picked him up in my arms. I sent some healing magic through him.

"I don't know who you are or where you're from, but you can leave him," said someone in the crowd. "He doesn't need healing."

Nobody was worried about him. I felt a rage flicker inside of me at the speaker's tone of voice and I turned to face them.

"But he's injured!" I said. "What do you mean I can just leave him?!"

"He's a healer. Look at him. He's dirty, sure, but he's not hurt, right?"

"Huh?"

I looked down at the boy again. He looked beaten up, but when I rubbed his cheek, I realized they were right—he was dirty but unhurt.

"This boy . . . He's . . ." I stuttered.

Is he really a healer?

Amako's words rang in my ears: "He couldn't help me, and I couldn't help him."

I had a feeling I finally knew what she meant by that. I looked down at the unconscious boy with a deep look of concern and realized that I had stepped into the darkness of the Luqvist School of Magic.

Amako
Informal wear
Travel wear
Felm

▲ Travel wear

▲ Travel wear

Gladys
▲ School badge
Halpha

Aruku
Welcie

Kiriha
Kyo

ONE PEACE BOOKS

The Wrong Way to Use Healing Magic Volume 2
(CHIYUMAHO NO MACHIGATTA TSUKAIKATA -SENJO O KAKERU KAIHUKUYOIN- Vol. 2)
©KUROKATA 2016
First published in Japan in 2016 by KADOKAWA CORPORATION, Tokyo.
English translation rights arranged with KADOKAWA CORPORATION, Tokyo.

ISBN: 978-1-64273-232-0

No part of this may be reproduced or transmitted in any form or by any means, electronic or mechanical, including photocopying, recording, or by storage and retrieval system without the written permission of the publisher. For information contact One Peace Books. Every effort has been made to accurately present the work presented herein. The publisher and authors regret unintentional inaccuracies or omissions, and do not assume responsibility for the accuracy of the translation in this book. Neither the publishers nor the artists and authors of the information presented in herein shall be liable for any loss of profit or any other commercial damages, including but not limited to special, incidental, consequential or other damages.

Written by KUROKATA
Art by KeG
Translated by Hengtee Lim
English Edition Published by One Peace Books 2023

Printed in Canada
1 2 3 4 5 6 7 8 9 10

One Peace Books
43-32 22nd Street STE 204 Long Island City New York 11101
www.onepeacebooks.com